SANTA ANA PUBLIC LIBRARY

3 1994 01480 9039

D0355125

For more than forty years,
Yearling has been the leading name
in classic and award-winning literature
for young readers.

Yearling books feature children's
favorite authors and characters,
providing dynamic stories of adventure,
humor, history, mystery, and fantasy.

Trust Yearling paperbacks to entertain,
inspire, and promote the love of reading
in all children.

THE
ISLAND
STALLION
RACES

BY WALTER FARLEY

A YEARLING BOOK

Published by Yearling, an imprint of Random House Children's Books
a division of Random House, Inc., New York

If you purchased this book without a cover you should be aware that this book is stolen
property. It was reported as "unsold and destroyed" to the publisher and neither the
author nor the publisher has received any payment for this "stripped book."

Text copyright © 1955 by Walter Farley
Text copyright renewed 1983 by Walter Farley and Random House, Inc.
Cover illustration copyright © 2003 by John Rowe

All rights reserved. No part of this book may be reproduced or transmitted in any form
or by any means, electronic or mechanical, including photocopying, recording, or by any
information storage and retrieval system, without the written permission of the publisher,
except where permitted by law. For information address Random House Children's Books.

Yearling and the jumping horse design are registered trademarks of Random House, Inc.

Visit us on the Web! www.randomhouse.com/kids

Educators and librarians, for a variety of teaching tools, visit us at
www.randomhouse.com/teachers

ISBN: 0-394-84375-4

Reprinted by arrangement with Random House Children's Books

Printed in the United States of America

May 2003

20 19 18 17 16 15

OPM

For Steve

CONTENTS

"Run, Flame! Run!"

1

The tropical sun was hot and brilliant. It made the open waters of the Caribbean Sea appear more blue than they actually were. It turned the golden, rounded dome of Azul Island into a flaming apparition. Yet its rays could not pierce the mist which hung like a gray veil about the base of this island of stone. Blue waters churned white going over the protective reef that lay a short distance out, then turned black as the waves gathered momentum and height to disappear behind the heavy shroud. They could be heard seconds later crashing against the walled barriers of Azul Island.

A lone boy guided the motor launch *Sea Queen* toward the perilous reef, his eyes never leaving the waters directly before him. He handled the wheel carefully, expertly. He watched the submerged coral slide past to either side of the hull. He seemed to know this particular area well. He piloted his launch in an ever alternating course, but one that took him always closer to the gray mist.

His name was Steve Duncan. He was no experienced mariner, for only recently had he been given the privilege and the responsibility of guiding the *Sea Queen* between the two islands of Antago and Azul, a distance of more than twenty miles. His home was in a small city in the United States, and he was on summer vacation from school. He wore a T-shirt and shorts. His body was deeply tanned from weeks spent beneath this hot, tropical sun, and the corners of his eyes were cracked with the white lines that come from squinting in the glaring sunlight for hours at a time. His black hair was cut short and uncovered.

He could have been any average and normal American boy . . . except for what he was about to do. In that respect, he did not conform to rule or type or standard.

He took the *Sea Queen* into the gray mist. If he heard the heavy thud of waves crashing hard against the wall of stone beyond, it did not seem to frighten him. He went in a direct line now. The engine throbbed noisily as though in protest to the mounting surge of the sea that would hurl it forward too fast. No longer could Steve see the dome-shaped top of Azul Island. He watched only for the precipitous wall that soon would rise a thousand and more feet above him.

Like the island itself, the approach foreboded danger. But Steve Duncan welcomed it, for it had kept all other people away. Now he began moving the wheel often again, and the propeller was reversed to steady the launch and hold it back from sweeping against the wall of stone that suddenly loomed ahead.

Steve had left the doors of the low sea hole open,

and now he skillfully took the launch through it and into the narrow canal which cut the floor of a large chamber within Azul Island. He moored the launch to moss-covered piles that were centuries old, and for a second he thought of the men from the Spanish galleons who had sunk them so long ago. Then he crossed the sandy floor of the chamber and closed the sliding partitions above the sea entrance. There was less light and wind now, but the waters in the canal still flooded and ebbed with the waves that found their way through the opening at the base of the hole.

Hurriedly Steve left the chamber and went down the tunnel which would take him to where he wanted to be more than any other place in the world. As his eyes became accustomed to the dim light he ran faster, never once looking at the coral rock in brilliant shades of pink, green, gray and white that had always attracted his attention before. Nor did he give another thought to the Spanish Conquistadores who had brought their men, weapons and horses along this path in their final flight from the English and French. For it belonged to the far distant past, and Steve Duncan was interested only in the present and the great red stallion who awaited him.

He emerged from the tunnel and entered a long chasm, not bothering to glance up at the sky above the close, sheer walls on either side of him. He ran faster, breathing easily but becoming very excited. Soon he arrived at a small sliver of a valley, and crossed the stream that cut its center. Still he ran on till he came to a rock-strewn gorge. There he slowed down to a walk, for the trail was jagged and twisting. He went down the dry river bed, following the gorge until he came to a wide patch of marshland. Here he went a little faster but he didn't run. He hated this particular area with its high reeds, swamp ferns and the thick vapors whose stench of rotting vegetation had been made worse by the sweltering afternoon sun. He held his breath as long as possible between short gasps of the foul air, his eyes remaining fixed on the narrow green swath of solid ground before him. He saw Flame's oval-shaped hoofprints and it made this part of the trip a little easier to bear. Soon he'd be with his stallion. There was only a short distance to go now.

Finally his path led upward, taking him from the hollow that fostered and nurtured the marsh. He began running again, leaving the dense vapors far behind. He climbed higher—and then, just beyond a field of wild cane, he saw Blue Valley! At the upper end a band of horses grazed. A few of them were drinking from a pool that was fed by a waterfall dropping a hundred feet or more down the precipitous wall.

Steve Duncan stopped then and whistled as loud as he could. In answer, a lone stallion emerged from the band . . . a tall chestnut horse whose mane and tail seemed to move like burning flame when he broke into a gallop. Steve ran to meet him.

No longer was the valley a place of quiet and peaceful solitude. The great stallion moved faster and faster over the short, thick grass, the beat of his hoofs resounding loudly from the walls of the natural amphitheater. He ran easily and without effort, his small head held high, his eyes never leaving the distant figure of the boy coming to meet him.

Steve entered one side of the field of wild cane as

the horse reached the other. He saw the stalks bend and break beneath the tall body of his horse. As he called and kept running, the red stallion swept by him, close enough almost to touch but without slowing stride. Steve did not turn back but ran faster through the cane.

When he had reached the grassy floor of the valley, he heard Flame behind him, and then the stallion thundered by again, running halfway down the valley before slowing. Steve watched him make his sweeping turn, moving from sunlight into shadows cast by the high western wall. Flame's great body was now shrouded with a clinging veil of blue, a color that the shadows picked up from the grass and coral rock.

And now Flame's call rose above the beat of his hoofs. It wasn't his clarion whistle of angry challenge. Soft and wavering, it hung on the air and welcomed Steve back home.

The boy laughed and kept running across the valley floor. He'd been gone only two days on this last trip to Antago but to him, as well as to Flame, it had seemed much longer. He was breathing heavily but soon he would stop running. He watched Flame sweep by him once more, and saw the short thrust of a foreleg as the stallion struck out in play without breaking stride.

Upon reaching the opposite side of the valley, Steve jumped onto a flat rock and then turned around, awaiting his horse. In only a few seconds Flame was beside him and he slid quickly onto the stallion's back. He gave no command. He barely had time to close his knees before Flame was off, stretching out as he had not done before.

Only twice during the long ride down the valley

floor did Steve call to him, and then he spoke softly into the pricked ears. "Run, Flame! Run!" He had learned long ago never to shout, only to whisper to Flame. He saw his stallion make for the band, the mares and foals scattering at his swift approach. Flame turned on winged hoofs and Steve shifted with him; then he went all-out up the valley and Steve had to close his eyes against the force of the wind Flame created. He pressed his head against the stallion's mane and neck. He was content to let Flame run as long and as fast as the horse liked. He'd know when the ride was over. But now he was *one* with Flame.

A half hour later he slid down from the sweaty back, as hot and wet as his horse. They were near the pool, and from all about them came the neighs of the mares. Flame had scattered them to the far corners of the valley by his playful but rough antics. Steve went to the pool and ducked his head in the cool waters. Flame joined him, snorting and lowering his small head to drink. As always, Steve marveled when after a few swallows Flame left the pool to rejoin his band. Hot as he was, thirsty as he was, this wild stallion would drink very little when overheated. Steve wondered how many domestic horses would have left the cool water as Flame had done.

Now too happy and tired to move, Steve stretched out on the soft carpet of grass. It had been a long hard day but just being back made everything all right again. What could be more wonderful than this? He had found that even the confusion of a small island like Antago bothered him now. He was well spoiled. But who wouldn't be, having found a lost world inhabited only by Flame and his band? It was a world free of every care except the care of horses.

Steve lay back, resting his head on his clasped hands, a long blade of succulent grass between his lips. He looked at the late afternoon sky with its light wisps of rippling clouds. The sun was well down behind the barrier walls, and Blue Valley was as blue as blue could be and very, very pleasant.

He supposed that if the day ever came when an airplane flew close to the dome of this island its pilot would know there was a valley down here. But the pilot would really have to be looking to find it. And where would such a plane be heading anyway? There was no land to the east as far as Africa, and the transatlantic airlines came nowhere near Azul Island. To the west there was only Antago, and no airline served that remote island outpost in the Caribbean Sea. Nor was there any nearby airport to service private planes.

Steve had no fear of discovery of his lost world from the sea. A few tramp steamers put in each year at Antago, but the more traveled sea lanes between North and South America were much farther to the east and west. Besides, no captain in his right mind would approach very close to Azul Island; it looked like a massive, egg-shaped boulder and was ringed by dangerous reefs. Small launches could get only to the island's small southern sandspit, and from there it was impossible to reach Blue Valley or even to learn of its existence. Natives of Antago said of Azul Island, *"Except for the sandspit it's nothing but solid rock."* Well, let them go on believing so.

Steve closed his eyes but quickly opened them

again. He didn't want to fall asleep. He had some work to do before it got dark. Pitch wouldn't be around tonight to help get camp in order and do the cooking. He wouldn't be around for many nights to come, for that matter. But it was as Steve had wanted it. He hadn't liked the idea of staying at Pitch's home in Antago while his elderly friend was doing his historical research in the New York libraries and museums.

Pitch had finally consented to Steve's remaining alone in Blue Valley, knowing full well that he could take care of himself. But he wasn't really alone, Steve reminded himself. He had Flame and the band. It was exciting being the only one on the island with them. Somehow it changed things a lot not to have Pitch around. Not that he'd ever seen much of Pitch during the daytime. Pitch had always been too busy exploring the maze of tunnels that ran through the coral rock of Azul Island. And when Pitch hadn't been on a tunnel exploration he'd been working on his manuscript, writing in detail all they'd found here and giving his reasons for believing that Azul Island was the last great stronghold of the Conquistadores, almost three hundred years ago! The Spaniards had left this natural fortress hurriedly, for all the relics Pitch had found indicated this . . . and as further evidence there were the horses which had been left behind. Where else could this pureblooded band have originated?

At this point in his thoughts, Steve sat up to look at Flame. Flame's forebears were Arabians of the finest strain. All one had to do to be convinced of this was to look at him and the mares. Their pure blood and the ideal conditions in Blue Valley had kept the strain free of flaw through generations of inbreeding. Now they were as perfect a group of horses as their ancestors had been . . . perhaps even finer.

Again Steve lay back on the grass, looking at the sky that was spotted with small, fleecy clouds. He was finding it difficult to keep his eyes open and began to realize that he must be more tired than he had thought. But he told himself that he mustn't go to sleep. He had time to rest after his long sea trip . . . plenty of time . . . just so he didn't fall asleep.

He listened to the splash of the waterfall and the occasional nicker of a mare to her suckling foal. Nothing else disrupted the peace and quiet of Blue Valley. Steve closed his eyes. Flame had come down the valley and was standing close by. Steve didn't have to open his eyes to know the stallion was there. Nor did he need to hear him. It seemed that the very air vibrated with the red stallion's greatness whenever he was around. If one looked, Flame's greatness could be seen in his eyes. But it wasn't necessary to look. One could *feel* it.

Steve suddenly felt a tightening in his throat, and he swallowed hard. Ordinarily he would have wanted Flame to be seen and appreciated by people other than himself, by horsemen who had never looked upon such a perfect stallion. But that kind of thinking wasn't for him, Steve knew. It wasn't possible for anyone but Pitch and himself to look upon Flame. To bring others here would mean the destruction of Blue Valley, the end of everything they held so dear. What they had here would last a long time. No one would know of Blue

Valley until Pitch had his historical manuscript ready for publication, and it would take him many years to complete that work.

Steve opened his eyes. Flame had taken another drink from the pool and was returning to his band.

Steve's thoughts turned to all the swift rides he'd had on Flame. Had there ever been a faster horse than his stallion? He sat up and watched Flame move from one patch of grass to another. His red body was scarred heavily from all his battles to maintain leadership of the band, but his legs were straight and clean of any serious injuries. He'd give any horse in the world the race of his life!

"Stop daydreaming," Steve told himself. "You have Flame and that's all that matters. Ride him as fast as you like here in the valley and let it go at that."

He looked up at the sky and decided to rest just a short while more before going to camp. He lay back again, closing his eyes and listening to the steady drone of the waterfall; the long moments passed pleasantly, easily, sleepily. . . .

Sure, he wouldn't change things from the way they were. But it didn't do any harm to imagine how things would have been under different circumstances. It didn't hurt to dream, to pretend that he was riding Flame in a great race back home. He could just see. . . .

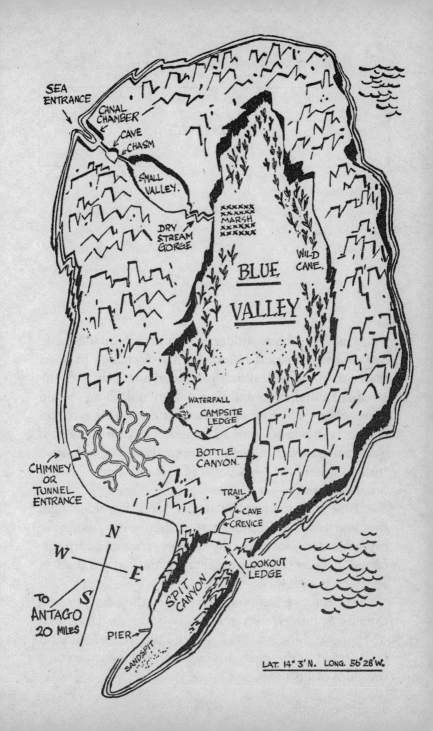

SEA
ENTRANCE

CANAL
CHAMBER

CAVE
CHASM

SMALL
VALLEY.

DRY
STREAM
GORGE

MARSH

WILD
CANE.

BLUE

VALLEY

WATERFALL

CAMPSITE
LEDGE

BOTTLE
CANYON.

CHIMNEY
OR
TUNNEL
ENTRANCE

TRAIL

CAVE

CREVICE

LOOKOUT
LEDGE

N
W   E
S

TO
ANTAGO
20 MILES

SPIT
CANYON

PIER

SANDSPIT

LAT. 14° 3' N.   LONG. 56° 28' W.

NOTHING

2

The great light came suddenly, so suddenly that it made Steve's eyelids smart before he had a chance to open them. And when he did, it was simultaneously with the screams of the mares and Flame. In that flashing second it was Flame's high whistle that made Steve's heart skip a beat, for never before had he heard anything like it! It was shrill but without defiance or challenge or welcome. Instead it held the worst kind of fear and terror, that of unknown peril.

Blue Valley was alive with a kind of golden light that had never before been seen there even under the brightest sun. Not even the deepest crag or fissure escaped. The light found everything and bathed it all in an awesome glow.

Steve looked up and saw the hurtling sun coming directly at him! He screamed, his terror matching that of Flame and the mares. Then he flung himself flat, his face buried in the grass, his hands pressed hard against the sides of his head.

A sun where there had been no sun. The end of the world had come!

His face unnaturally pale, Steve lay motionless, waiting for the end to come. In quick successive mental pictures he saw his mother and father, his home and Pitch and Flame. Then a heavy black curtain fell and he saw nothing at all. Seconds more he waited, perhaps minutes. From the smell of the earth he knew that he was conscious. He forced himself to use his ears, to listen. He heard the distant rush of the mares' and Flame's hoofs. Then he opened his eyes.

Blue Valley was as it had been . . . how long ago? Minutes? A lifetime? Had he imagined all this? No, of that much he was certain. He had only to look at the band and Flame to know. The mares had directed their suckling foals into the middle of a small tight ring they had formed; their heads were toward the center, their hindquarters ready to fling strong hoofs at any attacker. Outside the ring stood yearling colts willing to do battle but trembling with fear. Flame encircled the whole group, his eyes constantly shifting in every direction, his every sense alerted to the responsibility of defending his band. But he too was afraid because he could not *see* what threatened them.

The only brightness to the valley now came from the last reflections of the setting sun on the high eastern wall. There was nothing to fear or fight. Blue Valley was as quiet and peaceful as it had been before. *Before what?*

Steve sat up but did not attempt to get to his feet. He wasn't at all certain that he'd be able to stand yet. What had bathed the valley in that awesome glow? A meteor from outer space? He had seen shooting stars with long flaming tails in many a night sky. But never in the daytime or so close as this had been. He had read that most meteors were no larger than a grain of sand, becoming extinguished long before they reached the earth. But there'd been cases too of meteors so large that they resisted all the burning friction of the earth's atmosphere and fell intact, digging great holes in the ground.

Steve got to his feet and walked slowly to the pool, where he bathed his throbbing head. A meteor, then, was what it had been. It had almost landed on Azul Island. Where had it struck? Somewhere close, very close to the west. Now it must be at the bottom of the Caribbean Sea.

He turned to the band. The mares had broken their circle. But they were not yet grazing, nor did they allow the foals to leave their sides. With short, incessant neighs and nips they kept the long-legged colts and fillies from straying away.

Steve left the pool and climbed the narrow trail up along the end wall. Reaching a broad ledge that overlooked Blue Valley, he went into the cave behind it. Just within the entrance but far enough back to be protected against any driving rains were the stove, table, chairs and canned provisions. But Steve wasn't thinking of food. Whatever appetite he'd had was gone. He got one of the large lanterns, a flashlight and Pitch's binoculars. Then, leaving the cave, he continued up the trail until he reached the great opening where the underground stream rushed out from blackness to daylight, plummeting downward in a silken sheet to the pool far below.

For a second Steve stopped. He turned to look at

Flame and the band, then lit the lantern and went into the great opening. He walked to the right of the underground stream. Only when he rounded a long bend in the tunnel did he leave completely the light of day. He walked a little slower then, his hand occasionally touching the jagged rock on either side of him. Finally he came to a fork leading to many tunnels. Steve raised the lantern and saw the chalked figures and letters Pitch had marked on every wall of the explored passageways. Steve knew where he was going and how to get there, but he had learned to take nothing for granted in this underground maze. He made certain he had the right passageway before going on.

He continued for fifteen minutes or more, stopping only at intersections of other tunnels to cast the light upon the walls. His lantern bobbed from the short, mincing strides he had to take in the low-ceilinged passageways. If he hurried, he thought, he might be in time to look upon a sea still angry with the searing it had received.

Just ahead, a small square of daylight lay on the floor of the tunnel. Reaching it, he stopped and looked up the high ventilation shaft that pierced the stone. Pitch's rope hung down the shaft, but Steve had no intention of climbing to the outer ledge that was directly above him. He'd be able to look out upon the western sea without doing that. He began walking forward again, his head tucked between his shoulders, his back bent more and more as the tunnel became smaller. He went only a short distance before reaching the outer wall. There he extinguished his lantern, for three narrow slits of daylight came through the rock.

He looked through the middle slit first and saw nothing but the open sea. When he moved to the slit on the far right he could see the red sun resting on the water and just beginning its descent into the sea. For a moment he forgot everything in the beauty of the western sky. Seldom had he left Blue Valley to watch a sunset over the Caribbean Sea.

He blinked his eyes often in the brightness of the setting sun and suddenly realized that the glow from it was unusually strong. His gaze left the sun to search the waters around him for any vapors, any steaming bubbles to indicate that a flaming mass of molten metal had fallen. But he saw nothing of the sort so his eyes returned to the setting sun.

The huge red ball was now half obliterated by the sea, and the sky was aglow with all the colors in the universe. But the unusual brightness still marked the sun, and Steve blinked his eyes again. Once more he thought of the meteor. Perhaps it had struck directly in the path of his vision. Perhaps its steaming vapors were rising from the water and causing the golden glow that enveloped the brilliant red of the setting sun. He turned away, waiting for the sun to set completely so he'd know.

Minutes later the sun disappeared but the bright light on the water remained, *the same brilliant glow that had come to Blue Valley!* Steve told himself that it was being caused by gases from the meteor, still hot, still smoldering at the bottom of the sea. This was what he had hoped to see! This was why he had come! But although this made sense to him, there was no lessening to the pounding of his heart.

He squinted his eyes, hoping to see better. It was a nebulous, glowing mass of light and transparent, for he could make out the red sky directly behind it. Now he was certain it was produced by vapors rising from the sea. It was less bright than it had been only a moment ago. The meteor was losing its self-contained heat. The sea was crushing it, transforming it into nothing but heavy metal, fathoms upon fathoms deep.

Suddenly Steve thought he saw a movement within the golden mass. He tried to smile at this illusion but found he couldn't move his lips. Nothing was out there except vapors, he reminded himself. He reached for the binoculars hanging from his neck. Before he could get them to his eyes he saw another slight movement, then it too was gone.

He focused the binoculars many minutes before he became certain of what he had thought he'd seen twice before.

At first the object had no color or shape. Then as it became separated from the mass it appeared silver and needle-like against the background of red sky. It traveled downward, just above the water, and that was the last he saw of it. He didn't know if it had climbed back into the heavens or had sunk into the depths of the sea.

He was frightened but it wasn't the same kind of fear as when he had thought the end of the world had come. Never again would he feel such total, all-engulfing fear as that had been. It was as if he had suffered the very worst that could happen to anyone and, having survived, was stronger for it. Yet he didn't take his eyes from the glowing mass. He watched its brightness fade until it was nothing at all . . . only a small, round patch of grayish-white floating on the sea.

Steve held the binoculars up to his eyes until the world outside was as black as the tunnel . . . but even then he could tell where *it* was, for the patch was luminous. To anyone else it would have been nothing but the phosphorescence of a tropical sea. Steve knew otherwise. Something was out there! He turned and stumbled down the passageway.

Arriving at Blue Valley, he went to Flame in the darkness. He sought a return to normalcy in the familiar nearness of his horse. But, like himself, Flame was alert and watchful. The stallion's wild instincts told him that whatever had disrupted the quiet of his kingdom a short while ago hadn't gone. He wouldn't stray from his band that night. He wouldn't sleep or relax his vigil. And Steve knew that it would be no different for himself. But, actually, what had they to watch for? Neither knew, and that's what made the long hours to come so dangerous.

For the time of year, the weather that night was very unusual. No moon or stars were to be seen through a heavy, rolling overcast, yet only a few hours before the sky had been clear except for the flimsy lacework of rippling white.

Steve felt the chilling dampness, the nearness of the drenching rain to come. He moved closer to his horse, wondering if the heavens, like Flame and himself, were uneasy because of what had come to Blue Valley.

"You're being silly," he told himself, aloud and angry. Flame jumped away, startled by his voice. Steve called him back.

Over and over again he decided that what he had seen was only a meteor. He must accept that as a fact and nothing else. The meteor had sunk into the sea, leaving behind a bubbling trail that had created a great disturbance in the water *and in the air above it*. This had caused the golden mass, giving rise to his illusion of the three slender objects he had thought he'd seen but actually *hadn't*. The round, grayish-white patch that had remained on the water afterward was only something that had been created by the chemical reaction of gases and water. Tomorrow it would be gone.

Just then, and without further warning, the night rain came down heavily. Steve felt its rawness and decided that he and his horse were uneasy only because of the unseasonable cold. Suddenly he welcomed the rain, turning his face to the sky and letting it drench him thoroughly.

After a few minutes he told himself that he was being very foolish standing in the rain when it could lead to a bad cold and perhaps complications that would make it necessary for him to leave Blue Valley. "Pitch would really be angry if he caught me doing this," he thought.

Leaving Flame, Steve climbed the trail to camp. He went inside the cave and lit the stove for the warmth it would provide. He'd have a lot to tell Pitch. Pitch would never believe that Blue Valley had gotten so cold he had had to get the stove going to keep warm!

Steve removed all his clothes and rubbed himself hard with a large towel, then got dry clothes from the trunk and put them on. The rain was still coming down hard and cold currents of air swept through the cave.

He moved closer to the stove. He thought of having some hot soup, not because he was hungry but for added warmth.

Later he put the bowl of soup, half finished, to one side. He wondered at his lack of appetite. He was still shivering. He had brought no sweaters, no woolen clothes to the tropics. Then he remembered the light blankets and got one to wrap around himself. He didn't lie down, for he knew he couldn't sleep. He sat in a deep-seated canvas chair, watching and listening to the torrential downpour outside. It was going to be a long, long night.

Now, if Pitch were here it would be different, he thought. They'd watch the cold rain together and talk about how unusual it was. Pitch would insist upon having a big, hot meal. Afterward Pitch would sit beside him, smoking his pipe and telling about his latest tunnel exploration.

Steve closed his eyes so as not to see the rain any more. He would have liked to close his ears to it too. The rain wasn't helping matters at all. He wished that Pitch were there with him. He could have discussed with him all he'd seen at sunset, and then he would have been able to forget it and go to sleep.

Perhaps all he had to do was to pretend that Pitch was sitting over there in the other chair, listening. It wasn't hard to visualize Pitch with his bared, knobby knees covered by a blanket, his round face boyish and jovial despite his fifty-odd years. Pitch would be looking very serious, very intent.

And he, Steve, would be saying, "Pitch, the strangest thing happened today. For a while I was as scared as I'll ever be in my life, but now that I know what actually happened it makes a great story. There I was down in the valley with Flame when . . ."

Steve went to sleep with his lips moving, explaining to Pitch all that had happened at sunset.

THE NEW DAY

3

Steve awakened to a morning unlike any he had ever known on Azul Island. The air was so crystal clear that only the finest of fall days in the northern hemisphere could have been compared with it. Never had his valley been more beautiful; it was a sky-blue gem set in soft, warm, molten gold.

Steve breathed deeply and felt his whole being expand with the exhilarating air. It was as though he'd never really breathed before! Would Pitch believe this, when he told him? Would Pitch be able to imagine that a hard, cold rain such as they'd had the night before could wash the valley and air as never before, breathing new life into everything? Look at the horses! Look at Flame! They were frolicking, playing like young weanling colts, every one of them!

Listen to the birds! Where were they? Few birds ever came to Blue Valley and then they never stayed very long. They preferred the lush, green, volcanic islands such as Antago to the comparative coral-rock barrenness of Azul. Steve swept his eyes over the wild cane below, where the birds probably had gone in search of cover. He didn't see them yet their songs filled the valley, echoing and re-echoing from the walls.

There, up the trail! He saw them then, perched on the jagged rocks beside the waterfall. There were only two, but their incessant calls made it sound as though a whole flock of birds had migrated to Blue Valley.

Steve's gaze left them for the horses again. Oh, he had so much to tell Pitch! He wished his friend were here to share this morning with him. Never had he felt so well, so happy! There were so many things he *wanted* to do today. For a few minutes more he watched Flame frolicking with his band, the tall stallion stopping occasionally to press hard against the yearling colts. Flame did this not in combat but in play. The colts seemed to understand and they pushed back and rose with him, but never too strenuously, for they did not want to antagonize their leader. The day would come when these colts would fight Flame in earnest, teeth for teeth, hoof for hoof, in their attempt to take the leadership from him. But at their present age they were willing to play.

Steve turned away from them and went into the cave. He cooked a large breakfast of powdered eggs and milk and hot biscuits. While he ate he looked often at the gleaming valley and listened to the birds. He had plenty of company today! Not once did he think fearfully of what had happened the day before at sunset. It was something he was glad to have experienced. How many other people had seen a glowing meteor fall to earth? And wouldn't it add further interest to the written record he'd kept of his life on Azul Island?

Steve thought of the filled notebooks he had hidden away. They told of his finding Flame and the band and all the exciting times he'd shared with them. They were something he had kept completely to himself. Even Pitch didn't know of them.

When Steve had washed the breakfast dishes he wanted very much to share this glorious morning in play with Flame. But first he had some work to do. There was the stove to be cleaned, crates of provisions to be opened and stored away, blankets and clothing to be aired. There'd be time later for Flame, plenty of time, all the rest of the day.

For several hours he worked, emerging from the cave every so often to look at the horses. He always drove himself back inside. But the desire to play was very strong on such a day! Finally he was finished except for getting a fresh supply of water. Picking up a bucket, he climbed the trail. The birds, still perched beside the waterfall, flew away at his approach. He was sorry that he had interrupted their song.

One, a bright blue bird with crested head, dove headlong down the wall, not leveling off until just before he reached the pool. The other, a mottled brown-backed bird, was less daring. He glided down, circling several times before coming to rest.

Steve made a mental note to get an accurate description of them for Pitch, who'd probably tell him that the previous night's wind and rain had swept these birds to Azul Island from Antago.

Steve got his water from the rushing stream and then returned to the ledge. Now for Flame!

The red stallion and the band had stopped their

play and were grazing. The air remained crisp and cool even though it was almost noon. This had never happened before, and Steve marveled at it. Even the marsh at the far end of the valley wasn't sending up its foul vapors as it usually did at this time of day. He looked for the birds but couldn't find them. He hoped he hadn't scared them away. They belonged with this lovely day.

Steve whistled to Flame and the red stallion came loping toward him as he hurried down the trail. Flame stopped a short distance away, neighed and tossed his head, his heavy forelock falling over his eyes.

"Come on," Steve called.

The stallion shook his head but finally he came forward.

Steve gathered Flame's forelock. "I keep braiding this so you won't go blind trying to see through it, and you keep loosening it somehow," he said, laughing. "Stand still now, and we'll do it over again."

Flame tossed his head when Steve had finished, and the braided forelock moved up and down like a thumping whip. Steve slid onto the stallion's back.

Flame didn't bolt as he had done the previous afternoon. He stood restless but unmoving, awaiting commands from Steve's legs. Finally the light touch came and he went off at a slow gallop.

Steve kept Flame at that gait for a long while. They went down the valley, circled the band and came back. It was a day meant for riding and Steve intended to make the most of it. Just to be astride his horse, to be alone with him, was more than he could ever want.

But that wasn't exactly what he had thought yesterday, he reminded himself. Hadn't he wanted Flame's greatness to be appreciated by others? Hadn't he once again daydreamed of racing Flame? Yes, he admitted all this and he knew the reason for it.

Steve recalled the colorful poster he had seen in the Cuban air terminal during his long flight from the United States to Port of Spain, Trinidad, on his way to Azul Island well over a month ago. He had read it with great interest, as he did anything that had to do with horses. The poster had announced the running of an International Race to be held in Havana, Cuba, August 3rd. That was now less than a week away, he figured. The race was "OPEN TO THE WORLD"—and beneath this screaming declaration was a huge drawing of the globe.

Steve remembered boarding his plane again, wondering if "Open to the World" included Azul Island. So even then he'd been daydreaming of racing Flame! Such a fantastic prospect must be on his mind to a greater extent than he had realized.

Suddenly he heard the whir of feathered wings, and as a bird flew close overhead he saw the flash of the white under-body, the large blue wings and the crested head. It was the bird that had dived so recklessly down the end wall. The smaller, brown-backed bird was flying near the cane, squeaking loudly as though in warning or reprimand to the other.

Suddenly the blue bird flew in front of Flame and then downward, almost in the stallion's path. Flame thrust out a foreleg without breaking stride. He did it not in play but in anger. The bird annoyed him.

Steve, aware of Flame's mounting fury, turned him away from the cane, but the bird followed. Steve let

Flame gallop faster and the tall stallion welcomed the opportunity to leave his winged tormentor behind. His strides became longer as he swept across the valley floor.

Steve's clucking matched the rhythm of his horse's hoofs. As the beat became faster and they left the bird behind, he thought once more of the poster he had seen. He pretended that he had Flame on the Havana race track. *Steve Duncan racing Flame!* He bent closer to his horse's neck and told him to go on. Now they were passing all the other horses in the International Race. Now they were really moving!

They swept down the valley floor and as he neared the pool Flame began his wide, sweeping turn. Steve leaned with him, urging him to still greater speed. Now they were entering the homestretch. *"Come on, Flame! The finish wire is just ahead!"*

As the stallion lengthened out a low blue streak cut in front of him. Flame slowed his strides and struck out viciously. He even swerved aside, striking again at the bird who had dared to come so close to his legs. This time his hoof grazed the bird's long tail and the feathers flew. The bird dove into the tall cane, then rose again to be joined by his brown-backed friend whose high, squeaky calls of reprimand could be heard above the pounding of Flame's hoofs. After circling, the birds flew away.

Steve buried his head in Flame's flowing mane again, glad that the blue bird had left them alone. The stallion picked up stride and once more the valley echoed only to the beat of winged hoofs.

Minutes later Steve slowed his horse and circled

the band. Finally he stopped and slipped off Flame's back. He walked toward the mares but did not go close enough to frighten the foals. He sat down on the grass and waited for the mares to come to him.

He did not have long to wait, for the adult members of the band had accepted him long ago. The mares came closer but the suckling foals stayed behind their mothers, a little timid, a little afraid. It was they whom he wanted to make his friends. Every day he spent a short while with them, trying to win their confidence and acceptance.

He called to these long-legged, furry-coated sons and daughters of Flame, waiting for them to lose their shyness and come to him. But today they showed no curiosity over his presence and did not move from behind their mothers' protective bodies. Steve waited a long while before finally giving up. He got to his feet, regretting that he had made no progress.

On the way down the valley he passed a group of yearling colts at play. He called to one of them but the colt took no notice of him. This was the one whose broken leg he had cared for the summer before and whom he had intended to take home. But his parents had given him the choice of using the money he earned each year to maintain a horse of his own *or* continuing his summer visits with Pitch, and he had chosen the latter. He couldn't give up Flame and Blue Valley.

Steve walked on, aware that he didn't feel as well as he had only a short while before. Perhaps it was due to the blunt rebuff he'd received from the foals and the yearling colt . . . especially the colt, for they had been such fast friends the previous summer. The colt had grown up and away from him during the months he'd been away.

He brushed the sweat from his face, realizing suddenly that the weather too had changed. The sun's rays had finally penetrated the cool air of the valley. No longer was the day crystal clear but heavy with tropic heat. Steve decided, as he approached the end wall, that the afternoon was no warmer than any other in the past. It was just oppressive by comparison with those wonderful earlier hours.

Returning to camp, he made himself a sandwich, and stayed within the cave to eat it. Finally he rose from his chair and went out on the ledge to stand in the sun again. He felt the beads of perspiration come to his forehead, but he didn't leave the open ledge. His eyes and feet shifted uneasily as he looked down the valley.

Somehow, just as the weather had changed so had he. He was restless, even becoming concerned again about that floating white patch on the water. It was all so silly, so foolish. There was no reason to be concerned. He had decided once and for all it was something that had been caused by the chemical reaction of gases and water. It would be gone by now, swallowed by the sea just as the meteor had been.

He walked from one side of the ledge to the other, still ignoring the relief from the sun which the cave offered him. If it was the floating patch that was bothering him, why not make certain that it had long since disappeared? If his mind would not listen to reason, the only way to rid himself of his apprehension was to go and look again. He'd find nothing, and that would make everything all right.

Taking his knapsack and lantern, he went up the trail. The valley was very quiet; it seemed that the birds too had sought refuge from the heat. He hoped they hadn't forsaken Blue Valley altogether. It was nice having them around, even if the larger one had annoyed Flame. He turned to look at his stallion and the band. They were grazing in the shade of the western wall. Flame moved restlessly from one patch of grass to another, raising his head every so often, ears pricked and listening.

Steve went into the great opening, wondering if Flame felt the same anxiety that he did. And if so, for what reason, when everything had been so serene before? He hurried along the underground stream, anxious to reach the lookout post over the western sea.

When he arrived there he pressed his eyes close to the narrow slit. The afternoon sun was higher than during his last visit, so its rays did not obstruct his view of the sea's surface. He saw immediately that the grayish-white patch was still there, and the blood began pounding in his temples. He pressed his head closer to the stone, welcoming its coolness. He tried to make sense of what he was seeing. It must be floating algae, phosphorescent at night, grayish-white during the day. But why then hadn't it moved? Why was it anchored in the same identical spot as last night?

He forsook the coolness of the stone against his head for the binoculars and the better view they would provide. As he put the glasses to his eyes, he found that his hands were moist. He chastised himself, ridiculed himself for his mounting concern. But nothing helped.

He looked through the binoculars. The patch was no different than when seen with the naked eye . . . it was grayish-white, round and motionless. Steve stayed there a long while, not wanting to leave without having decided once and for all what it really was. He didn't want to spend another uneasy night.

He could not have told how long he had been there when he saw some sort of a stirring directly above the patch. He told himself it was being caused by the sun's rays. But the sun was still high in the heavens. A light was beginning to dance directly above the grayish-white patch. Rapidly it became brighter, and then Steve knew what it was. *The golden mass of the day before. The second sun that had swept over Blue Valley. The meteor that was no meteor!*

In a few seconds the mass was big and round and glowing. Steve closed his eyes against its brightness. Yet he didn't keep them closed, for he wanted to watch. He saw the long flash of an object high above the golden mass before it plummeted down to the water. He made out its needle-like shape just before it disappeared within the great light. Then the mass faded rapidly until nothing was left on the water but that small patch of grayish-white.

Steve lowered the binoculars, turned away and staggered through the tunnel. What was out there on the water? What had he seen?

Whatever it was, he and the horses were safe in Blue Valley. Nothing, *no one* could reach them within the barrier walls of Azul Island. Soon *it* would go away, and all would be quiet and peaceful again. But what was it? He wanted to *know*.

His breath came faster just as his steps did, without his being aware of it. The needle-like object that had flashed through the sky had been guided to that mass of golden light, he decided. Guided by whom? What was the light? Where had it gone?

He stumbled and fell, but managed to keep his lantern from being broken. For a moment he lay on the ground, finding comfort in his familiarity with this underground world. A soothing quietness came to his body and mind. Perhaps he had seen nothing at all. Perhaps his eyes, affected by long weeks of bright, tropical sun, had created these optical illusions of mass and objects. Mirages had appeared to others at sea and in the desert. Why not to him?

Finally he got to his feet and began walking again. But he had gone only a short distance when suddenly he fell to his knees with a force that sent the lantern crashing hard against the jagged wall. The strong current of tunnel air quickly extinguished the flame and then he was in total darkness.

He made no attempt to get the flashlight from his knapsack but remained absolutely still, listening. Yet the voices could not be real, nothing he actually heard! His ears, like his eyes, he decided, must be playing tricks on him in this black world a thousand and more feet beneath the dome of Azul Island.

On hands and knees he went forward, feeling his way along the ground. The voices rang constantly in his ears, soft and almost musical, *clear and so distinct.* Was his mind too playing tricks on him? No one else could be in this maze of tunnels known only to Pitch and himself!

He inched forward, rounding a turn, and there he saw the light of a burning lantern coming from a side chamber. He dropped flat on the ground so quickly that his head struck the stone, the impact making the blood gush from his nose. But he felt nothing, saw nothing . . . only his ears seemed alive.

"Really, Jay," a voice said impatiently, "it's getting late and we should go back. We've wasted most of the day already."

"Wasted?" another voice asked. "Did you expect to find anything like this? You know as well as I do that we're most fortunate."

"Well, of course. I admit all that. But at the same time we mustn't overdo it. After all, there's work to be done."

"It can wait."

Steve raised his head, listening to the voices and experiencing a strange solace in his final acceptance that they were *real*. No longer did he have to fear discovery with no chance to fight back. The danger was here, only a few feet away from him. He rose and went slowly forward, making no noise. He tried to still the pounding of his heart, afraid that it might betray his presence. Closer and closer he moved to the doorway, stealthily transferring his weight from one leg to the other. Not once did he take an awkward, uncertain step or dislodge a loose stone. Every movement was fluid, coordinated and planned. Fear stole silently along with him, but this fear he understood and accepted. It was as real as the voices of the men within the chamber. When he was almost at the doorway, he stopped and listened. The waiting had come to an end. Now he would know what he must face to protect himself and the horses.

"Come in, Steve," one voice said suddenly. *"We've been waiting for you."*

THE STRANGERS

4

The words came as unexpectedly as an unseen blow, almost striking him down as he stood there rigidly, his back against the side of the tunnel. He had felt so certain he could not have been seen or heard.

"Please, Steve, come in," the voice repeated. "We really don't have much time." It was not a command, only an impatient but gracious request.

But Steve had no intention of entering the chamber. And, finding that his legs had lost their temporary immobility, he moved quickly. He knew where this tunnel would take him and he planned to lose his pursuers forever in this world of darkness.

His hands were raised to ward them off if they sought to stop him when he passed the doorway. But they weren't there. A swift glance disclosed that they were well to the rear of the room, one sitting on the edge of the chamber's lone table, while the other stood beside it holding a lantern.

Steve came to a sudden stop, telling himself they

could never reach him from where they were or travel the tunnels as fast as he. But what made him stop was more than that. It was the men themselves.

They were no taller than Pitch, who was a short man, and they were just as thin and light-boned. But it was their clothes that startled him most of all. They were dressed more for a northern business office than a tropical expedition, much less one to the rocky depths of Azul Island. Their suits were heavy and newly pressed with knife-edged creases. They wore fine shirts and bow ties.

As Steve looked at them they stared back, their gazes unwavering and interested. Their faces were round and, like their voices, soft and gracious. There was nothing evil or sinister about them. They smiled at him and then were silent, as though waiting for him to speak.

Steve gripped the jagged stone of the doorway, ready to pull himself away at a run. He must not be influenced by their appearance. He must not step inside the chamber, where they might catch him.

Finally the one holding the lantern said, "I *do* wish you wouldn't take so much time, Steve. We must be getting on."

The other slid easily from his seat on the table. "You're always taking so much for granted, Flick," he reprimanded. "Can't you see that Steve is startled at finding us here? First, we should introduce ourselves." He came across the room, his hand outstretched. "My name is Jay, and . . ." He stopped abruptly when he saw the boy draw back from the doorway. "Don't go, Steve. Please don't go. Are you really so frightened by us?"

It was impossible for Steve to say anything. He could only look at them, wondering who they were and how they had ever gotten there. The eyes of the man standing only a short distance away from him were crystal clear and yet had color. More than anything else they promised him no harm. Yet Steve said not a word, nor did he relax his muscles.

"Flick," the man said without taking his eyes off Steve, "please bring the lantern over here. I want to talk to Steve, and one *can't* talk to a person in the dark."

As the other came forward with the lantern, Steve was about to run but he checked the impulse. The two men were now within a few feet of him, but they were still far enough away for him to be able to elude them, he decided.

The man who had brought the lantern spoke. "Really, Jay, this is all taking much too long," he said impatiently. "Let's try again some other time. We're neglecting our duties."

"Nonsense. Just relax, Flick. I'll attend to everything, and it won't take very long."

"No," the other answered. "You're too impetuous. I'm in charge, remember that."

Steve turned from one to the other. Far from being sinister, these two men were arguing like a couple of children. He looked at them again in the bright light of their lantern. The one called Flick wore a brown tweed suit, a white shirt and a black-and-gold tie. His hair was gray and cropped short; it had a bright reddish tint, and yet the small mustache beneath his large beaked nose was more black than gray or red. Steve found it impossible to be alarmed by him.

The other man wore a sky-blue suit, a white shirt and a black string bow tie. His hair was very long and wavy, more blue than black. There was nothing frightening about him, either.

"Careful," Steve warned himself. "That may be what they want you to think. Don't let them come closer."

Jay's gaze was still on him. Steve glanced at the man called Flick and found the same shimmering clearness of eye, devoid of all color yet containing all the colors in the world. He felt a sudden throbbing in his head.

"Aren't you surprised to see us, Steve?" Jay asked again. "You're more startled than frightened, isn't that so?"

Steve nodded as he felt a numbness claim his body. He fought it, telling himself that he should run, but he couldn't leave. He could only stare into those eyes, thinking how much they resembled glass marbles. And yet they looked back at him as marbles never could, with more expression than he had ever seen in anyone's eyes.

The men waited patiently, kindly, while he tried again to speak. They came no closer . . . but even if they had, he could not have left.

They were helping him, and finally his words came in a whisper. "How did you get here?"

Both smiled, and it was Jay who answered. "Why, in our ship, of course. You've seen it, Steve. You've been watching us right along."

"We're just over there," Flick added, nodding his cropped gray head to one side.

Steve turned his head toward the wall of the chamber, and Flick chuckled and said, "Of course I mean *outside*, Steve."

"There you go taking too much for granted again," Jay said disapprovingly.

Flick's small mustache trembled in his irritation. "I wish you'd stop saying that, Jay. It's all I've heard from you during this trip. You know as well as I do that there's only so much we can tell Steve."

"Oh, nonsense," Jay retorted. "You're always worrying about nothing. No wonder you're gray long before your time. And wearing that ridiculous crew-cut doesn't fool anyone, either." He turned quickly to Steve, not wanting to give Flick an opportunity to speak just then. "Steve," he explained, "we're on the water out there. We arrived late yesterday afternoon, and of course we knew that you were watching us. We realize how concerned you've been. Please don't be any longer."

Flick said, "Actually, we've been just as concerned about *you*."

Jay nodded his blue-black head in agreement. "That's one of the reasons for this visit. I don't believe we've ever been seen before. It's quite . . ."

"Now, now, Jay," Flick interrupted nervously. "You know what Julian said."

"Worrying, always worrying, you and Julian. Just leave it to me to know how much to explain."

"I've tried that before and it hasn't worked out very well," Flick answered gravely. He turned to Steve and smiled. "You mustn't mind our bickering. This has been going on a long time."

"Too long," Jay said. "The next trip will be different. I'll team up with Victor."

"They won't have it," Flick answered. "You and Victor are too much alike." He shrugged his thin shoulders, adding, "But it would be perfectly all right with me. In fact it would be a pleasure not to have to worry about you at all."

Steve realized vaguely that none of this could be real. He couldn't be thousands of feet deep within the walls of Azul Island, listening to these men argue as they might have done in any living room! It couldn't be happening, *and yet it was.*

Finally Jay turned to him again. "I suppose old Flick is right in a way, Steve. Maybe you'd better just accept our being here. It'll be easier on you. Of course you know about our ship, having seen it. Unfortunately, it takes us a little while to cool down after a long voyage . . . friction, you know. But we never dreamed anyone would be at this remote spot to see us come in."

They were talking about the golden mass of light, only it was more than light. It was their ship and it was still there, above that small grayish-white patch, without being visible!

Sudden alarm passed through Steve like an electric shock, shattering the numbness that had brought immobility to his legs. He moved them now, seeking to turn and run.

But their hands caught him quickly, keeping him still, and he knew he could not get away, that all hope of escape was lost.

Flick said casually, "So little has missed Steve's attention. Really, it's most remarkable. He's even seen the cruisers."

"So he has," Jay returned. "But I don't think it matters. Steve has as much to conceal as we do. He's a very unusual person."

As Steve listened, there flashed through his mind all he had read about the frightening, secret weapons of war that were being developed and tested by countries throughout the world. Was this ship one of them? Were those needle-shaped objects he'd seen even now bent on the destruction of distant cities? This was very real and *deadly*!

"Look at us, Steve," Jay said.

Only then did Steve realize that Jay and Flick had been silent for many minutes. He made a great effort to focus his eyes upon them, to see them as they actually were. He *had* to know the answers to his questions.

They were looking at him, but neither spoke. Their features had become so blurred it was difficult for Steve to make them out. He tried to blink to clear his vision, but found he could not move his eyelids. The two faces grew more and more indistinct until they were blotted out completely. Only the shimmering light of their eyes remained and that shone brighter and brighter, seemingly enveloping him in an intense heat.

Steve knew that he could not fight this growing inner warmth, that all he could do was to welcome it. Stronger and stronger it became, flooding his body and very being till there was no room left for fear or suspicion. He felt only a deep sense of comfort and confidence and trust.

How long it was before he could see their faces again, he could not have told. But suddenly he was asking himself how anyone could look at these two men and think anything but good of them. Flick was smiling, pleased and happy that Steve trusted them completely, that he now felt confident no one, no country, had anything to fear from them. Jay, too, was smiling, even chuckling.

"*Now,* Steve," Flick said softly, "I was wondering when you and Pitch first found this place."

"Pitch! Do you know Pitch?" Steve asked aloud, surprised at their mentioning his friend's name, surprised even more that his words came so easily.

"Oh, no," Flick answered hastily, ". . . just a little *of* him." He glanced at Jay with fleeting concern.

"Who told you about him?" Steve asked.

"Well . . . well, *you* did, Steve." Flick turned to Jay helplessly.

"There you go getting yourself into a jam," Jay said, "and wanting me to get you out of it. I told you before that if you start something with Steve you must finish it. You just can't let it hang in the air. He won't have it."

"He's only a boy," Flick answered defiantly.

"Of course, and that's exactly what I mean, Flick. We're not dealing with a closed, inflexible, adult mind here. Young people *are* different, Flick, and we might as well accept that right now. We must get used to having Steve ask questions that I believe no one but a young person *would* ask. And really, Flick, it's going to make our visit much more fun."

"But, Jay . . ." Flick began.

Jay ignored him and turned to Steve. "Getting back to your question about our knowing Pitch, Steve. As Flick started to say, *you* told us about him. What I mean is that you've been thinking about him right along and we're able to tune our minds to yours without much trouble. It's something on the order of what you'd call telepathic power, I believe. But it's simply an exchange of thought messages, which we've taken great pride in doing for a long, long while." He chuckled, then added, "However we don't overdo it, Steve, for fear we'll lose the use of our voices. Now let's talk about Flame. While we were watching you ride him this morning we . . ."

"Y—you mean you know about Flame too? You were in the valley this morning?"

"Yes to both questions, Steve," Jay replied. "As Flick mentioned a few minutes ago, we were concerned about your having seen us. Naturally, we thought it best to check up on you." He straightened his black string tie and smiled, hoping to relieve Steve's anxiety. "Of course everything is all right, perfectly all right *now*. It's just that we didn't know what to expect."

Flick nodded his cropped head in full agreement, and Jay went on, "But let's talk about the horses, Steve. Flame is a very beautiful animal and you sit him well."

"Can't you get your mind off horses, Jay?" Flick asked in a bored tone. "That's all I've heard from you since we arrived."

"I'm sorry but that's the way I feel about the subject," Jay answered brusquely. "My interest in horses is nothing new, as you very well know."

"I know. I know," Flick said resignedly. "You certainly have a well-balanced mind, ninety percent horse, I'd say. I should have known better than . . ." He stopped abruptly, and raised the lantern to Jay's face. Then he went on, "It's just occurred to me, Jay, that you might have known there were horses on this island when you picked our landing site. After all you were at the controls at the time."

"Oh, no, Flick," Jay said, hurt. "This is just as much of a surprise to me as it is to you."

"How did you get in here?" Steve interrupted the argument.

Jay smiled. "Oh, we have means of leaving the ship," he replied casually. "You've seen us."

Steve thought of the cruisers they'd mentioned. Even now one of those slender objects must be somewhere within the barrier walls of Azul Island . . . probably in the smaller valley near the sea entrance.

Flick came around Jay to join in the discussion. "And then of course we followed you into the tunnels, when you went to look at our ship again. We stopped to rest when we came to this chamber, knowing you'd return presently."

"That was your idea," Jay said bitterly. "I wanted to go ahead and surprise Steve."

"I'm glad you didn't," Steve spoke up.

Flick said, "We'd better be getting back now, Jay. I'm sure it must be very late."

"Julian is there. He'll take care of things."

"But it's *our* job," Flick insisted. "The others won't like it."

"We're late now, so they're angry already," Jay answered. "A few minutes more won't change things." He turned to Steve. "I'd like a cup of tea, Steve. You do have some, don't you?"

Steve nodded and obediently followed them out of the chamber. He marveled that they knew their way through the tunnels but he was not surprised. One's mind could take in only so much and his had had its fill. Later he'd find out all he needed to know. From what country had they come? What manner of people were they to have built an airship that could not be seen while anchored and were so far advanced in the power of telepathy that they knew about Pitch just from his having thought of him?

He continued walking close behind Flick, who led the way, the light bobbing before him. He felt no fear or suspicion of them, only the confidence and trust that had come to him in the chamber. This, too, had been their doing. Otherwise wouldn't he have been afraid for himself and the horses?

When they emerged from the tunnels and stood beside the waterfall, Blue Valley was in deep shadow. The air was very cool and pleasant, much as it had been that morning.

Jay glanced at him and said, "Lovely, isn't it? And you'd like it to remain this way?"

Steve nodded.

Jay winked and said, "Sometimes weather can be a state of mind, Steve . . . like a lot of other things."

Flick gave Jay a stern look of reprimand as they started down the trail.

It took only a few minutes to get the canister of tea Pitch had stored away and to have the water boiling. Jay balanced his cup of tea on the fine crease of his blue pants. "Let's talk about Flame, Steve," he said.

"Not now," Flick interrupted. "Make it another time. Drink your tea and let's go."

"You'll be coming back then?" Steve asked.

"Of course, Steve," and Jay chuckled. "I wouldn't miss this for anything." He looked at the table behind Steve. "May I have one of those biscuits?" he asked.

Steve passed the can to him. Jay had taken only a bite when Flick rose from his chair, his face red with anger.

"You're being most difficult," he told Jay. "You know you'll get plenty to eat when we get back. I've taken enough of your lack of consideration." He pulled Jay from his chair and forcefully led him down the steep trail.

Steve watched them go. After they had reached the valley floor they walked across to the field of wild cane. Flame was grazing in the distance, and Steve wondered if he should warn his departing visitors that the red stallion would not tolerate strangers in his kingdom. Almost at once he decided it was not necessary to warn them . . . yet he wondered why he felt so certain of this.

It was becoming quite dark, so he could barely see the two men. They were directly across the valley from Flame, and yet the stallion never stopped his grazing. Like everything else that had happened, Flame's lack of vigilance was unbelievable. Even though Flame might not be able to see the two strangers in the darkness, he should have been able to sense their presence.

Steve felt the cool night air on his face. Moments passed, and then the two men were gone. Steve stayed where he was, his gaze shifting to the sky above the dome of Azul Island, watching for a thin streak of silver. He waited a long while without seeing anything.

Finally he looked down at the plate that held Jay's half-eaten biscuit. If it were not for this bit of evidence, he would have found it hard to believe the two men had actually been there.

Suddenly he heard a noisy outburst from the birds.

They were above him as they had been early that morning, perched on the rock beside the waterfall. The large blue bird was closer, and as usual was more bold and boisterous. Apparently he had seen the biscuit and wanted it, for he flew down and came to rest a short distance away.

Steve tossed the biscuit outside on the ledge. The bird dove quickly, snapping it up with one hard thrust of his bill.

As Steve watched him fly off with the biscuit, he regretted having given away his only tangible evidence of the last weird hour. It was all too fantastic to believe! He looked up at the night sky and saw nothing but the two birds in flight. A chill swept over him. It was all a dream, wasn't it? Nothing had actually happened. There were no such persons as Jay and Flick.

"... ALWAYS WORRYING ABOUT NOTHING"

5

Steve cooked a large meal. He opened tins of beef and peas and carrots and onions. He used garlic and herbs, trying to remember all that Pitch had told him about preparing a savory stew. Actually he was not hungry, although he knew that once the food was before him he would eat. To keep busy was his main objective. He did not want to think about his strange visitors any longer.

When he finally sat down to eat, he found the stew not at all to his liking and not at all like Pitch's. Too much garlic. Too much thyme. But he scarcely paused between mouthfuls. It was as though he were willing to do anything, anything at all, to keep from thinking. The next stew would be better, he told himself. He'd been experimenting. He'd learned a lot. The next stew would be better. He'd go easy on the garlic, easy on the thyme.

Later he heated water and washed the dishes and pots. He dried them slowly, not certain what he could find to do next. He looked outside the cave. The evening sky was clear. There would be no cold rain tonight to chill him, no shivering. He heard the soft neighs of the mares calling their colts. Flame was quiet. There was not a sound from him, not even a hoofbeat.

When Steve had finished doing the dishes, he walked onto the ledge, where he could see the dark silhouettes of the band. His eyes followed their movements but his thoughts wavered and then rushed headlong past every mental barrier he had erected to keep himself from thinking of Jay and Flick. Surely their being here meant the destruction of all he held so priceless!

Why was it that he was so alarmed now, when he had willingly accepted them without fear only a short while ago? Was this the aftermath of all he had seen and experienced? Was *this* reality and the other a ghastly hoax, a scheme by which Jay and Flick had somehow warped his mind, making him see good where there was only evil?

He thought of the airship that had swept through the heavens like a second sun and had come to rest, invisible, on the water. Surely this craft with its slender cruisers was the most advanced, most secret weapon in the world! Jay had said he didn't believe it had been seen before.

If the United States had developed it, he'd surely be taken to Washington. And if it belonged to another country, a potential foreign enemy, he might be . . . Steve walked restlessly about the ledge, the skin drawn taut and white about his high cheekbones.

Was it any wonder that he was fearful, when all his life he had heard and read of the hatred among so many countries of the world? Was it not the reason for great standing armed forces and the fantastic advancement of secret weapons? Had he not seen with his own eyes the most powerful weapon of them all?

He stopped walking and told himself to forget all he had read about prejudices and misunderstandings between governments. If he thought only of Jay and Flick as they were everything would be all right again. He could trust them completely without preconceived suspicion and hatred, without alarm or dread, regardless of what country they were from.

For many minutes he stood still, trying to visualize their faces. How hard it was to form a mental picture of them! How long had they been gone? An hour, two hours at most.

He could remember details, their suits and shirts and ties, Jay's heavy hair that was more blue than black and Flick's short cropped head and small black mustache. But he couldn't put everything together and say to himself, "This is Jay . . . and that's Flick." No matter how hard he tried he couldn't form a mental image of their features, and he wanted so much to look into their eyes again. He knew that if he were able to do this, the inner warmth and trust would come once more.

He began walking again, making every effort to bring their faces to mind. But only an indistinct blur of faces resulted, not old, not young . . . real and yet not real. Finally, frustrated and angry with himself, he lay down upon his cot.

Looking up at the night sky, he thought, "At least I can remember that there was nothing sinister or evil about them. I know they were good faces, kind faces. Besides, how could anyone have listened to Jay and

Flick argue like a couple of small kids and still be afraid of them? Jay was so irresponsible while Flick acted like the worst kind of a worrier, constantly reminding his friend that they were being neglectful of their shipboard duties. And Flick had gotten so angry when Jay said, *'No wonder you're gray long before your time. And wearing that ridiculous crew-cut doesn't fool anyone either!'*"

Steve laughed and closed his eyes. He had a teacher back home who wasn't unlike Flick in that the older he got the shorter he had his hair cut and the louder became his clothes.

It was good to be able to laugh, to have confidence that he would get everything straightened out the next day and that there was nothing at all to fear. He settled down in the brisk coolness of the night, as did the mares and Flame in the valley below.

Early the next morning the red stallion stretched out his long legs to the greatest of strides. His hoofs hardly touched the cropped grass before he lifted them again, taking Steve down the valley with a speed that made the walled amphitheater much too small and confining.

As always when his horse was in full run, Steve had no alternative but to move forward over Flame's withers, his knees pulled high to keep from falling off, his hands and head on the stallion's neck. A silhouette would have revealed only the outlines of the horse, for Steve's position never changed, even when Flame swept into sharp turns that took him across the valley and into the borders of the cane before he straightened out again.

After a long while Flame's strides shortened. He

slowed to a gallop and then finally to a walk, his body white with lather. When Steve slipped from the stallion's back he was as sweaty as his horse. He pulled Flame's head down toward him, breathing heavily. Suddenly a voice from behind said, "You should keep a hot horse moving, Steve!"

Steve whirled around to face Jay, then looked beyond.

Jay smiled and said, "I got away *alone* this time."

Steve shifted his gaze back to this man, who came and went without his seeing him. Eagerly he scrutinized Jay's face. Why hadn't he been able to remember it last night or this morning? It seemed so easy now. Soft and kind, a most common face. But somehow Steve knew he'd never remember it once Jay had left him again. For it was real and yet not real. The eyes had color and yet were crystal clear without color. The skin was white and yet not white, without blemish—not even a stubble of beard—and ageless.

Finally Jay broke the long silence. "Nothing accounts for more hind end lameness than *standing* a hot horse. You'd better walk him, Steve."

It was strange that only then did Steve think of Jay's nearness to Flame. Quickly he turned to his horse. No fire burned in Flame's eyes. The tall stallion looked past Jay, seemingly unconcerned over the stranger's presence.

Steve didn't move. He couldn't take his eyes off Flame, so astonished was he at the stallion's easy acceptance of Jay. He heard the man say, "Really, Steve, I've seen more good horses ruined by trainers doing just what you're doing now! Flame should be sponged off with warm water, swiped, blanketed and walked for at least an hour."

Steve answered, "Flame's used to this. He'll cool himself out. He won't stand still."

"Really, that's too much to expect of any horse, Steve," Jay said with concern. "Please walk him."

Steve touched Flame, and the stallion moved toward the pool.

Jay began to follow Flame, but then returned to Steve. "I dislike interfering like this, Steve. I really do. I know you're well able to take care of your horse. But believe me, Flame shouldn't be allowed to drink any water now. Why, that's even worse than his standing still! He'll founder himself. He'll get cramp colic. He'll die!"

Steve laughed at Jay's outburst and said, "Watch him."

Flame wet his long nose and left the pool, walking down the valley.

Steve added, "He knows how to take care of himself. They all do. That's all they've ever known . . . they and their forebears."

Jay said nothing, but he didn't take his eyes off the constantly moving stallion. Finally he sat down on the grass, pulling up his pantlegs to keep the fine crease in his blue suit. "I suppose you're right, Steve, but I wouldn't take any chances." He looked up at the boy, and then back at Flame. "Especially after such a hard ride as you gave him," he added gravely.

"You watched us?"

"Of course, Steve. There's nothing I enjoy more than getting up early, before dawn sometimes, and getting to a convenient track to watch horses in training. It really does something for me!"

Steve looked down at this well-dressed man who might have been at a popular metropolitan club, telling friends of his visits to Belmont Park or Churchill Downs. Yet here he was, where so few had ever been, very much at ease and urging him to sponge Flame, to blanket him, to walk him. . . . Flame, a wild stallion!

"I just wouldn't want anything to happen to him," Jay said. "He's too fine a horse. I've never seen a better one. You must do everything possible to keep him sound."

In the distance Flame lowered himself carefully to the grass and began rolling, his long limbs cutting the air.

"You sit him beautifully, Steve," Jay said without taking his eyes off the rolling horse. "No one could have a better seat. It wouldn't get by in a show ring, of course, but on the race track it's the only way to ride."

"I've never raced," Steve said.

"I know," Jay replied quietly.

Steve continued standing. He couldn't sit down beside Jay and chew thoughtfully on a succulent blade of grass as the man was doing. He was not sufficiently at ease for that. He wondered how it was that Jay knew he had done no racing. Perhaps he would be able to find out. He was aware from having listened to him yesterday that Jay loved to talk and that it wouldn't be long before he knew a lot more about this man and where he was from.

"Do you know why you have the ideal racing seat?" Jay asked.

"No. I just try to keep from falling off."

Jay laughed loudly, and his hair fell low on his forehead when he shook his head. He turned quickly to the boy, only his eyes smiling now. "I wasn't laughing at you," he said when he saw Steve's flushed face. "Your saying that reminded me of what happened a short while ago. I was down South on a visit when . . ."

"South America?" Steve asked quickly.

"No. Southern United States," Jay replied. "Kentucky, I think it was, but it's not important. Anyway, I was watching the horse races at a small country fair and most of them were being won by kids riding bareback. There were a couple of big Eastern trainers there, and I got talking to them. It seems they went to the small fairs looking for horses they might be able to use on the big city tracks. They were disturbed because while they'd been buying a lot of the winning horses at the fairs it turned out that they didn't run very well when they reached the Eastern tracks. The trainers couldn't understand what happened to the horses' speed."

Jay stopped, and his eyes glowed with an unusual brightness.

"Maybe it was the faster competition," Steve suggested.

"No, it wasn't that at all," Jay answered. "The reason was that the trainers took the horses but left the kids who had ridden them behind."

"Were they such good riders?"

"In a way," Jay replied thoughtfully. "You see, those kids at the fairs didn't have enough money to buy saddles, so in riding bareback their first objective was to keep from falling off." He smiled and then went on, "A simple matter of self preservation, Steve, as you pointed out a moment ago. They hung on to whatever was best to keep their balance. They moved forward over their mounts' withers. They pulled up their knees and leaned close to their horses' necks, holding mane as well as rein. In doing all these things their weight was forward, where it should be for extreme speed, and in addition they cut down wind resistance to a minimum; their bodies didn't act as a brake."

Jay paused to glance at Flame, who was walking slowly around the band.

It gave Steve a chance to say, "But certainly that's the way jockeys ride even with saddles."

Jay turned quickly to the boy. "Oh, no, Steve. You're mistaken. I've watched them. They ride with very long stirrups and sit straight up in the saddle with their weight in the *middle* of a horse's back. Really I can't understand why they do it! They just don't seem to use their heads at all. It makes me a little angry, especially when I think of what happened in England not long after my visit to that country fair."

Steve said nothing. He knew that the crouched forward seat of riding had been first introduced to horse racing well over a half-century ago!

Jay continued, "I was spending only a few days in England, but naturally I visited the track every morning. And, Steve, listen to this. One morning I saw the trainer I'd spoken to at the country fair, and working for his stable was one of the boys who had ridden bareback! I realized immediately that this man had finally come to his senses. I told him as much and he agreed fully. His boy was using a saddle then, of course, but his seat was exactly the same as it had been while riding bareback at the fairs.

"Now what disappointed me so greatly was this," Jay went on sadly. "Even though the boy was winning more than his share of races over the long-stirrup, middle-of-the-back type rider that's currently so popular, his crouch style was being ridiculed in England. His trainer confided to me that he felt the reason for the public's non-acceptance of the boy and his excellent style of riding was because he wasn't *'fashionable'*!"

Jay paused, waiting for Steve to say something. But Steve was too bewildered to move his lips, much less able to get any words out. Anyone who had read the history of horse racing knew that the great American jockey Tod Sloan had successfully introduced the popular crouch style of riding in England as long ago as *1897*!

"Aren't you surprised, Steve?" Jay asked. "Doesn't it make you furious too?"

Steve finally got his words to come. "I don't know what you mean by 'fashionable,' " he said.

"I believe the trainer meant that it was because of the color of the boy's skin. He was black. His name was Billy Sims. Yes, I believe that's what he was called. So many things happened during that hurried trip, and all were so very *new* to me. Although as I said it was only a short while ago, it's difficult for me to remember some of the terms and language usage."

Steve could not take his eyes off the man who sat on the grass in front of him. And when he spoke, he did not recognize his own voice. "Y-you s-said all this happened a short while ago. Do you remember the year?"

"*Your* year? No, I'm afraid not, Steve. I'm not very good at that kind of thing. But wait. Let's see now." The blue-black head suddenly turned, the clear eyes alive and dancing. "Why of course! I went to the Doncaster Sales and saw that beautiful gray colt sold. I've carried his picture in my wallet ever since. I clipped it from a magazine. It may give the date."

A long wallet was drawn from the inner pocket of the striking blue suit, and then Jay read the clipping silently. Finally he said happily, "Eighteen ninety-five, Steve."

A short while ago to Jay. But to anyone else, well over a half-century!

When Jay saw the expression on Steve's face a somber curtain fell over his bright eyes and he spoke with concern. "Something I've said has startled you, Steve. Tell me what it is. I don't want you to be frightened of me."

"I–I'm not frightened," Steve heard himself say. "It's just that it h-happened so long ago."

"Really? In your time, you mean?"

Steve could only nod, and Jay said, "I suppose I should have thought of it. Details like that always escape me." The shadowy darkness left his eyes and the brightness returned, greater than before. "Then the crouch style of riding is now being used in racing horses?"

Steve nodded in still greater bewilderment.

"Oh, how I wish I could see them go! To think that I have to stay near the ship. The pity of it!" And then the man's eyes were no longer bright but blood-red in sudden anger. "It was Flick who insisted that we visit

Mao rather than *Earth.* He said so little had changed here since my last visit. The blackguard!" he shouted bitterly. "The scoundrel! No doubt he knew of this all along! So what did he do, Steve? What did he do? . . ."

Steve's face had whitened; his head seemed too heavy to move.

"I'll tell you what he did," Jay went on. "He excited my interest in Mao by telling me of some horses that inhabited that planet. And what did I find? Scraggly, flea-bitten animals that were no more horse than I . . . *or you are,* Steve," he added hastily. "Oh, the imbecile he is, not to know a horse when he sees one! And then he takes me on a great tour of the oceans of Mao, the most boring trip of my life. Nothing but colored water! And when I think what was awaiting me here, why, Steve, I could just . . ."

He stopped and the anger left his eyes while he studied the boy's face. Finally he said, "Why, you're *surprised,* aren't you, Steve? After yesterday I just took it for granted that you had figured out who we were."

Steve's tongue felt too thick for speech.

"Not that Flick or the others would approve of my telling you this in so many words," Jay went on. "They're always worried that people will be frightened if they know about us, and then we won't be able to come back again. I think that's all rather silly, don't you?"

When Steve did not answer, Jay continued. "Oh, I'll admit that if you saw us as we really are you'd probably be frightened. Of course there wouldn't be any good reason for your fear, but that's the way you are.

Sometimes I find it difficult to understand, and I try. . . . I really do, Steve. It seems you're always jumping to conclusions without thinking things out. Oh, I don't mean you personally, Steve," he added quickly. "You're doing fine, just fine. It's your people I'm talking about . . . your *adults.*"

Jay glanced toward the valley where he could see Flame. "And I don't mean to infer that this is true only so far as we are concerned. Take your own kind. Take Billy Sims. His was only a difference of skin color, as I understand it." Jay's gaze returned to Steve. "But, as you've reminded me, that was all many years ago. I'm sure the people of your world must be more understanding of each other in every way now. Aren't they, Steve?"

Steve looked at the face before him, but no words came. *Then it wasn't real.* And yet the eyes that weren't eyes at all found his own, holding him forever. Would they make him accept all of this that he was being told in the most casual way, as one friend talking to another? He stared back into the glowing, bottomless pits and an eternity seemed to pass.

Meanwhile he was asking himself, "Is what I've heard more fearful than what I dreaded last night, the secret weapons of war and foreign enemies? Isn't what I know to be *real* more dangerous, more deadly and vicious than this, which I consider *unreal*?"

Jay said, "Don't think about it any more, Steve. I have your answer, and I'm sorry to hear it."

It was the overpowering disappointment in Jay's voice that startled Steve even more than his remembering that nothing could be kept from this man, not even one's thoughts. *But Jay wasn't a man.*

"Oh, but I am, Steve," the sad voice came again. "Perhaps I'm not exactly what you think of as a man, but I am one, all right. You want to know what I really look like? Well . . ." He paused to study Steve, and at the same time ran a hand through his hair. "I guess we'd better not go into that, Steve. Not that you don't have a very open mind, but really there's no reason for my showing you. One form is as good as another, we've found. It's what a person *is* that counts. We learned so long ago to change from one shape to another that it comes almost automatically now. It's simply a matter of taste and convenience at the time."

He stopped abruptly. "You're not really frightened by what I'm telling you, are you, Steve?" he asked with grave concern. "Just surprised, perhaps a little startled?"

Steve got his head to nod. The truth was that he *wasn't* frightened. No matter what he was being told, he couldn't look at this man with the troubled eyes and be scared.

Jay laughed in a pleased way. "I knew you wouldn't be frightened, Steve! I knew it the moment I first saw you riding Flame. You were so carefree, so happy with your horse, wanting only to share the morning with him! I told Flick as much. I really did. But he and the others are such old 'fuddy-duddies,' Steve. They didn't believe me at all. They're so afraid to divulge anything to *anyone.*"

Jay shrugged his thin shoulders. "But then I suppose it's because they never really got together with a boy before. I told them that it's entirely different than dealing with an adult. And I'm right, I know I am. Just the short time I've been with you makes me very, very certain of it. Oh, you're skeptical of everything I've told you about us, and wary too. But the point I'm trying to make, Steve, is that *inside* where it counts you've accepted us even though it's contrary to everything you've ever known or been told. Thank heavens for your youth, Steve!"

The man bounded to his feet in quickening enthusiasm. "At your age, Steve, I believe I could help you in many ways if you'd only let me. I've always said that it could be done if we found the right open-minded person." Jay paused and a bold and eager light blurred his features. "We can try it *now*, Steve, but it won't be easy. You'll have to listen to me very carefully. No closed mind now, not one bit of it!"

Desperately Steve tried to raise his head above the heat that was fast enveloping him. He sought Jay's face, but nothing was there except an indistinct shimmer of light . . . that and the blue-black hair, a black string tie, a white shirt, a blue suit. His hands shot up to his eyes, covering them so he could not see the dancing light. *"Do what? What do you want me to do?"* he heard himself ask in a voice that did not seem to be his own.

Still eager and with overwhelming curiosity Jay asked, "Would you like to *fly*, Steve? It's the easiest thing and the most fun of all. Listen to what I have to say now. You must relax a bit more and help me. Make your mind a blank. Forget everything you've ever known in this world you call Earth. Forget all you've ever seen and been told. Now, Steve . . ."

Steve felt a heavy blackness come swiftly to his mind, claiming it for its very own. He fought it as he had never fought anything before. There was no pain but he writhed in agony and his arms flayed the air, fighting nothing. He opened his mouth to yell, but no sound emerged.

"You're *thinking*, Steve." Jay's patient words came to Steve from somewhere deep within the recesses of his brain. "You're thinking of all you know as *normal*. Don't let it come to that, Steve. Shut it out of your mind, and just listen to me.

"You *want* to go on with this experiment. I know you do, for I can feel it so strongly. Don't let what you've been told through the years stand in your way. Push it out, Steve . . . push . . . push . . . don't let it take over. I realize it's strong for it's all you've ever known. Don't let it come between us, please *don't*."

Steve fought all the harder, seeking to drive the blackness away. An overwhelming desire to see Blue Valley and the horses again had risen within him. He felt it surge stronger and stronger as he fought against the dark void that Jay would have him enter. Yet there were long moments when he was confused by his fighting, for he was willing to go with Jay.

The blackness lightened a little, and he didn't know if he was glad or sorry. Where was Flame? He had to see his horse! He struggled more furiously, forcing the dark void further back with all the will he possessed.

Jay's voice came again, disappointed now. "I guess I was wrong, Steve. Some other generation, perhaps, but not yours. What your mind has absorbed as normal is much too strong for me, even though you *did* want to cooperate."

When Steve emerged from the darkness, his first responsive reflex was to shout. His voice, throttled for so long, split his clenched lips and shattered the quiet of the valley. When it had died, the sound of Flame's swift hoofbeats could be heard. But from closer still came Flick's angry voice.

"I knew you were up to something, Jay, the moment I found you gone." Flick stood beside Jay, his eyes as angry as his voice. "You can't do this to Steve," he went on. "Mark my words, your conduct this morning will be reported to Julian!"

"You and Julian," Jay replied quietly, ". . . always worrying about nothing."

A Matter of Convenience

6

As the sound of rhythmical pounding grew louder Steve turned away from the men and saw Flame coming down the valley, his ears back, his nostrils spread wide in fury. For a second Steve thought how easy it would be to say nothing, just to stand still and allow Flame to destroy Jay and Flick and the nightmare they had brought to Blue Valley. But was that what he wanted, *now that he knew who they were?*

He looked at them again, and from somewhere deep within him came a sudden cry of warning. *"Run!"*

They turned toward him, startled by the urgency in his voice. But Jay continued sitting on the grass, making no attempt to get to his feet. It was Flick who turned around and, seeing the oncoming stallion, shouted and ran.

Jay looked back, then scrambled to his knees and with the speed of a sprinter followed Flick. Both had reached the rocky trail before Flame swept past Steve.

The stallion came to a halt at the wall, his eyes

large and red. He screamed at the men above him. He rose high on his hind legs and pawed the air in his fury and frustration. When he came down he bolted along the wall, sending large clods of earth flying behind him. Then he turned and came back, running like a caged animal, his anger never abating.

Steve made no attempt to quiet Flame. Instead, he kept looking at Jay and Flick, who were seated on the trail, breathing heavily and scared. They were safe because Flame would never attempt the steep climb, regardless of his fury. They could have been two normal people who had run from an enraged animal. But they weren't. They were men from another world. Steve waited and watched them, thinking of all he had been told and what Jay had attempted to do to him.

"Would you like to fly, Steve? It's the easiest thing and the most fun of all. . . . Forget everything you've ever known in this world you call Earth."

For long minutes Steve's gaze was fixed on the two frightened figures huddled together on the trail above Flame. Seeing them so afraid helped him more than anything else. For if he accepted their fear as the kind of fear that was normal in his own world, mustn't he try to think of what he had been told by Jay as normal in *their* world? His head throbbed. Would there come a time when even the people of Earth would be able to . . .

"I guess I was wrong, Steve. Some other generation, perhaps, but not yours."

He had his answer.

Flame came to Steve, and his wide nostrils began to close as the anger ebbed from his giant body. He had understood Steve's shout and the danger that had threatened him but not the reason for it. Now he heard the boy's voice, soft and caressing. He listened, his ears no longer flat against his head but pricked and alert to every sound. He felt the comforting touches on his neck, and the fingers that ran from his mane to his fore-lock. He lowered his head still more, and stood quietly, very docile and content. He knew everything was all right now. Not that he understood the words, but the rhythm of the sounds and the soft touches comforted him. Finally he was told that he could go to his band, if he liked. He stayed a moment more and then left, moving up the valley at a slow gallop.

Steve went to the trail. Jay and Flick got to their feet when he neared them, their eyes as sheepish and em-barrassed as those of two children who had run away, leaving another behind to fight in their defense.

Flick was the first to pull himself together. He turned angrily upon Jay. "You see! You see what you did! We might have been killed!" he accused the other.

Jay shrugged his narrow shoulders in an attempt to appear casual. "Flame took me by surprise or we wouldn't have needed to run. After all, I've had *some* ex-perience with horses."

"I don't mean only that," Flick raged. "You were told to leave Steve alone, and if you think for a moment that I'm going to forget this . . ."

"Now, Flick, now," Jay said calmly. But suddenly he turned to Steve as though he were remembering his experiment for the first time. "Ah, Steve . . ." He paused and began again. "You're not angry with me, are you? After all, you really *wanted* to try it."

Steve looked at this little man in the blue suit who

now was perched above him, having passed Flick in his frantic climb to get away from Flame. He stared into eyes that in spite of all their wonder and knowledge were as troubled as a small boy's, asking forgiveness. Steve shook his head.

Jay smiled and turned to Flick once more. "There, Flick," he said. "Steve's not angry at all!" He paused and then added bitterly, "I don't see why you're getting so upset."

"Nevertheless, I'm reporting this to Julian," Flick answered. "You were told to leave Steve alone, and you disregarded your instructions."

"What about Mao?" Jay asked. The tone was soft, but the expression in the eyes was hard, stony. "Weren't you told to confine our trip to the seas alone?"

Flick blurted out something that Steve couldn't hear, but he saw the back of the cropped gray head turn uneasily.

"You wouldn't, Jay. You *couldn't*," Flick said, loud enough for Steve to hear him. "After all, that was a side excursion in the interest of the *arts*."

Jay smiled. "You're so sensitive to the beauties of art and nature, Flick," he said. And then Jay no longer smiled. "But so indifferent to the practical matter of getting along with *people*!" He glanced sidewise at Steve and added, "My chat with Steve here was on that order . . . creating a mutual understanding of each other and our different ways of doing things."

Steve turned away from Jay to watch Flame and the band. But after a few seconds he felt compelled to turn back to Jay and Flick and listen to every word they had to say.

"After all," Flick was saying, "the Mao incident was such a little thing, Jay. Really nothing at all."

"My chat with Steve was just as little," Jay returned quietly.

They kept standing there, looking at each other. Finally Flick repeated, "You wouldn't tell Julian, Jay. You *couldn't.*"

"You wouldn't, couldn't either," Jay said. "If you'll forget about this morning and give me a little more cooperation than you have in the past, I'll forget Mao." He grinned broadly at Steve, disclosing his small, white teeth. "Let's continue this discussion over some tea," he suggested. "It's just what we all need to soothe us down."

Steve followed them to the ledge. He put the water on to boil, and then got the tea. "This is Pitch's tea," he told himself, his fingers tightening about the can. "It's imported and costly. He's going to be sore when he finds so much of it gone." And then he laughed at the absurdity of his thoughts, considering what he was going through.

Flick said crossly, "Well, Jay, I suppose it *is* too late to do anything about you and Steve now. I'll simply have to assume full responsibility for your actions, as I've done before."

Jay chuckled. "That's the ticket, Flick. Handle me *yourself* without any help from Julian. You're perfectly capable of doing the job, and there's no sense getting Julian mixed up in it."

Flick said nothing.

The water boiled and Steve made the tea extra strong, the way Jay liked it. Flick came up and stood beside him, holding out his cup.

"Since Jay told you as much as he did it's only right that you know more about us," Flick said. "The little information he's given you can be a very dangerous thing."

Steve was not aware if Flick's words were being spoken aloud or not. It didn't matter. All he knew was that he heard everything in the softest, most rhythmic cadence and that he understood it completely.

He poured the tea into cups. "Would you like a biscuit?" He laughed inwardly. Did he imagine for a minute that this was a party, that friends had come to tea? He passed the biscuits around and thought of the one Jay had not finished the night before.

"Oh, but I did," Jay said, smiling. "But I'll have another if you can spare it, Steve. Thank you very much."

Steve stared at Jay a long time, thinking, *The blue bird had dived quickly, snapping up the biscuit with one hard thrust of his bill, and then had flown away.*

Flick ran his fingertips through his stiff brush of hair, and then said, "I believe the best way for us to explain what we are, Steve, is to say that we're simply tourists." He turned to Jay. "Don't you think so?"

"You're the scholar," Jay answered. "Explain it your way, now that you've consented to take Steve into our confidence."

The coolness of the morning swept in a sudden wind across the ledge. Steve rubbed his bare arms to warm them, but felt no chill, no shivering. . . . That would come later, after his two visitors had gone.

Flick said, "Well, we'll just call ourselves tourists, then. We travel a great deal, Steve, truly great distances as you know them."

"You mean as he *doesn't* know them," Jay interrupted, laughing.

The sound of Jay's laughter startled Steve, for now he knew why it had sounded so familiar to him all along. It was like the raucous call of the blue bird. He turned to Flick and asked, "Where are you from?"

"Our world is called Alula," Flick answered. "It's not too unlike your Earth."

"As far as the geological features go," Jay interrupted again.

"Of course," Flick said sharply, "that's all I meant."

Jay smiled. "And it's cooler. That's why we prefer a day like this."

Steve rubbed his chilled bare arms again but said nothing. He thought of the cold rain the first night Jay and Flick had arrived and wondered whether they had preferred that too.

"But we don't have your sunsets," Flick said. "Never have I seen a more glorious one than on the night of our arrival! Why, the sky had more color than the seas of Mao. Didn't you think so, Jay?"

"Let's not talk about Mao," Jay answered sullenly. "When I think of what that trip has kept me from seeing here, I could just . . ." He stopped, and a band of red appeared in his eyes. "Why did you tell me there was so little change on Earth, when you knew of my interest in horses? *Why*, Flick?" Jay had risen from his chair and was standing over Flick.

"But I didn't know of any great change," Flick insisted nervously.

Jay waved a long, bony finger in Flick's face. "Do you mean to tell me that during your last trip here you never noticed jockeys crouched forward in their saddles, their knees pulled up?"

"Of course not," Flick said defiantly. "You know I never go to the races."

"But you *heard* of this new racing seat, didn't you?" Jay insisted. "After all, you're supposed to be the scholar, the well-informed person who knows what's going on, even in the most remote of planets!"

Flick looked at Steve helplessly, and then threw up his hands. "One can't possibly remember *everything,* Jay! Perhaps I did hear of this new riding style, now that you've mentioned it. But I didn't think it was important. There are so many other things that . . ."

"Not important!" Jay shouted, and then he put his head in his hands, rocking it. After a moment he turned abruptly, went back to his chair and sat down. "To think," he said softly, "that they had to assign an old man like you as my companion on this trip . . . one who no longer can appreciate the drama of a horse race, and in addition cannot retain a single important fact!"

Flick rose from his chair, the red band in his eyes also. He spluttered, finding it difficult to speak as he turned and looked at Steve.

This man old? Steve studied Flick's soft, lineless face and the hair that just now seemed to be more red than gray. "He's not old at all," Steve thought.

Suddenly the little man beamed and the angry red left his eyes. "Oh, I'm old, all right," he said appreciatively. "Still, it's nice to be told I'm not." Glancing over his shoulder, he added fiercely, "And you're just as old, Jay. Don't forget that."

"Not in *heart,*" the other answered.

Flick ignored Jay. "What's bothering him," he explained to Steve, "is that two of us always have to stay with the ship while the others go off touring. It worked out that our turn for ship duty came here on Earth."

"We could have traded with Julian and Victor," Jay said. "Julian wanted to visit Mao again, but you insisted upon *our* going instead."

"Julian might have traded, but not Victor," Flick said thoughtfully. "Victor really wanted to visit Earth. He'd never been here, remember."

"I wish Victor and I had been assigned together," Jay said wistfully.

"It wouldn't have worked," Flick answered. "Everybody knew that." He turned back to Steve. "You see, we use the 'buddy system,' as you do in your Boy and Girl Scout organizations. And it's for the same purpose . . . to keep track of each other, and to . . . ah, avoid trouble. One is supposed to have a restraining influence over the other. That's why Jay was assigned to me."

Jay snickered. "It was the other way around," he said.

"Look at it any way you like," Flick said, shrugging his shoulders. "But now we must get back to the ship."

"Why must we go?" Jay asked furiously. "You know the others won't be back for . . ." He glanced at Steve, ". . . a week, I guess it is in your time."

"We're not certain of that," Flick said quietly in the face of Jay's angry outburst. "Some of them might just change their minds and return sooner. Anyway, it's our job to be on the ship and keep everything in order. You're well aware that we mustn't shirk our duties."

"We can clean everything up just before they get

back. No sense working now when we can enjoy ourselves. After all, it's very unusual to have someone like Steve around."

"*Very,*" Flick admitted in the same soft, patient tone. "But they expect no less of us than we did of Julian and Victor while we were visiting Mao, even though . . ." He paused, his small eyes traveling over Steve, ". . . we are more fortunate."

"Nonsense," Jay muttered. "They'd be glad we had a chance to enjoy ourselves while still keeping an eye on the ship."

"Maybe so, but we still have our moral obligations."

"You didn't think of moral obligations when we were on Mao," Jay grumbled.

The red streak reappeared in Flick's eyes. "You promised not to mention that again," he said fiercely.

"I only promised not to report you to Julian, providing you'd give me a little more cooperation than you have in the past," Jay reminded him.

"Well, haven't I?" Flick demanded, his short hair bristling. "Doesn't Steve know more about us than anyone else has ever known?"

"You realize as well as I do that we don't have to worry about Steve," Jay returned quietly.

"Well, didn't I promise not to report your . . . *your experiment*?"

"Sure. Sure you did." Jay began moving down the trail. "All right, we'll go . . . but really you're not very adventurous, Flick."

Steve followed them down the trail. He knew they wouldn't allow him to witness their departure. He didn't understand how he knew, but it was there, somewhere in his brain.

When they had reached the valley floor Steve continued walking with them. He told himself that he was going to see Flame. But he knew that was not his only reason for staying close to Jay and Flick. He did not want them to go. There was still too much he wanted to learn.

They walked very quietly with their heads down. Perhaps, Steve decided, they were bothered by his presence. Perhaps they wanted him to leave now. But he would have *known*, wouldn't he? And nothing had as yet told him to go.

Jay suddenly broke the silence. "There's something else, Flick," he blurted. "I don't see why I shouldn't be allowed to watch just one race while I'm here. After all it would *only* be a matter of a few minutes to get to . . ." He stopped and turned to Steve. "Where'd you say that race was going to be?"

Steve just looked at him.

"Yesterday morning while you were riding Flame," Jay prompted anxiously. "You were racing him somewhere. Now where was it? You were going so fast that it was difficult to . . ."

"*Jay!*" Flick said, horrified. "You wouldn't make a trip, even a short one! You *couldn't*. Why, Julian would be furious!"

"Julian needn't know," Jay answered quietly. He turned back to Steve. "Where was it?"

Steve said finally, "Cuba . . . Havana, Cuba."

"Oh, yes," Jay said. "See, Flick, it wouldn't take any time at all. Julian wouldn't know, would he, Flick? After all, there are some things that don't need to be reported to him. Your side excursion on Mao, for example."

Flick's face was as taut as stretched wire; he said nothing.

They walked a few strides more, and then Jay grabbed Steve by the arm excitedly. "Why don't you and Flame come too, Steve? *You can race him!* That's what you wanted, wasn't it? We'd have plenty of room in the ship."

Steve could not have told how long he stood there in astonished, numbed silence. His only recollection of time afterward was hearing the sudden rush of Flame's hoofs. The stallion was coming up from behind them, his ears flat against his head, his eyes bright with anger at sight of Jay and Flick.

Steve ran toward Flame.

The red stallion slowed when Steve appeared between him and the men, but he did not stop. He swerved to one side and went on, his nostrils flared, lips pulled back.

Steve tried to swerve with his horse but tripped in his hurried, frantic plunge and went down hard upon his hands and knees. Picking himself up, he turned around. He was about to call to Flame when the sound died quickly on his lips. *Jay and Flick were nowhere to be seen!*

Meanwhile Flame had swept into the wild cane, seeking the men who had escaped him once before! His loud snorts shattered the stillness and his tall body cut great swaths in the waving field of green. He refused to give up his search, galloping in winding paths that took him back and forth through the cane.

Steve watched in silence, knowing that Flame's search was futile. His stallion was no match for Jay and Flick, any more than he was. Where had they gone, and how? Were they even now somewhere within that field of cane and, if so, in what form? Hadn't Jay said, *"We learned long ago to change from one shape to another. It's simply a matter of taste and convenience at the time."*

Turning his gaze skyward, Steve saw the two birds circling above the dome of Azul Island. He thought of the blue feathers of one, of the high-crested head and the splash of white. He thought of the other's brown mottled back, the long beaked bill, the bit of red on the head and the black mark beneath the bill. And then he sat down on the grass and successfully pictured Jay and Flick.

While Steve sat there, occupied with his thoughts, Flame came up and stood beside him. He was alert and ready to fight in the boy's defense. But he saw and heard nothing, even though he remained with Steve for some time.

"LAUGH, PLEASE"

7

Steve felt a tongue licking his forehead. He could tell it was not Flame's for there was no affection in the motion, only an eagerness to lick the salty beads of perspiration that covered his face and matted his hair.

He rolled over on the grass and at once the suckling foal ran to its mother and stood behind her large, protective body. "Come, Princess," Steve called softly to the mare.

The mare had been gray but was now white with age. Her body was heavy and sagging but there was nothing aged about her head. It was still small and fine and beautiful.

She was the oldest of all the mares, and for this reason Steve regretted having named her "Princess." She was more a queen, a proud dowager queen, and the filly by her side would probably be her last. But it was too late to change her name now for she knew it so well. Unlike the other mares, she would come at once in answer to his call, just as she was doing now.

When the white mare reached him she lowered her head so he might rub it. After a minute or two of this Steve rose to his knees, fondling the soft muzzle with the bristling hairs. "Good girl," he said. "Good old girl."

Flame stopped his grazing to watch them but stayed away.

Softly Steve stroked the mare, his fingers finding spots that gave her much pleasure and contentment to have scratched because she could not reach them herself. She lowered her head still more so he might rub behind her small ears. He held her close. It was good to be wanted, to be needed. . . .

He looked beyond the mare to the suckling filly, who stood quietly in the shadow of her mother's big body. Cautiously the filly peered at him from beneath the mare's tail, her eyes big and fuzzy in her curiosity and shyness. He called to her, "Come, little Princess."

The foal pricked up her small, furry ears at the sound of his voice, and remained so as he continued talking to her. The white mare nickered for more attention and shoved her head against his chest. Steve continued rubbing the mare but he spoke only to the filly. Finally she moved to her mother's side, her slender neck and head stretched out, trying to reach him without coming any closer. Her soft, large eyes gazed intently into his own; there was no wavering, no fear . . . just a girlish shyness. Her mother was accepting him, loving him, but the filly was still uncertain and very, very cautious.

Finally the filly took another step closer, her thin muzzle stretched out and trembling. Steve made no attempt to touch her. He waited for her to come to him.

And at last the mole-soft nose was on his cheek, the lips moving, searching and finally nipping. He drew back a little, for her milk teeth were strong, and continued stroking the white mare. Now the filly moved eagerly forward to pull at his shirt. She did not want to be left out of things. When Steve scolded her for tearing his shirt she drew back but did not run off in alarm. Instead her eyes glittered naughtily and she renewed her nuzzling.

Steve patted them both for a long while, and then found his eyes turning often to Flame.

"Why don't you and Flame come too, Steve? You can race him! That's what you wanted, wasn't it? We'd have plenty of room in the ship."

Jay's words couldn't be shrugged off as sheer folly! For how often had he dreamed of racing Flame? How many times had he taken him about the valley, pretending they were in a great race? Only yesterday morning he had pretended he was riding Flame at Havana. And Jay had known. How had he known? Where had he been? It was one thing to have Jay and Flick standing beside you, looking at you, knowing they were able to read every one of your thoughts. But it was something else to have them know so much when you were not even aware of their presence.

Steve remembered Flame's winged tormentor, who had flown about him during the fast ride and then had narrowly escaped being trampled by the stallion's powerful hoofs. Yes, Jay had been in the valley yesterday morning, and Flame had come close to destroying him.

Steve fondled the two heads in front of him, one so mature and wise, the other so young and eager. A cold wind was blowing and yet he was perspiring freely. He thought of everything Jay and Flick had told him, and then he said aloud, "It can't be true!" But inside, where Jay had said it counted most, he knew it was all very true and that he had accepted Jay and Flick and the world from which they had come.

"I know they're from a distant planet," he thought. "Is that so fantastic, when we've been told of the possibility of there being other peoples, other worlds in a universe so great it defies description? Therefore, I accept what they've told me of their world of Alula. I accept their world as being far older, far more advanced than my own. I accept Jay and Flick from that world, not as deadly, threatening enemies to our very existence, but as good and kind friends touring other worlds in much the same manner as we visit other states and countries. I accept all this, and having accepted it I have nothing to fear except what I've learned to fear in my own world."

Later that afternoon Steve got pencil and paper and sat down to write. Quickly he made notes of Jay and Flick and the ship, of everything he had been told, everything he had felt. He tried to believe that this was but another account of his life in Blue Valley . . . one that would follow in sequence the records he had hidden away. Only the others were nothing like this, nothing in this world could . . . He stopped writing, looked at the sky and repeated aloud, *"Nothing in this world."*

He had no chance to turn back to his notes just then, for a voice suddenly asked, "What are you writing, Steve?"

Jay was standing on the trail.

"You know what I'm writing, Jay," Steve said. "Why do you ask?"

The man chuckled. He came within the cave to join Steve, but he did not look at the papers. "It's more polite and sociable to ask, Steve," he answered. "After all, if we can't *talk* to each other . . ." He stopped, paused a moment and then went on, "You're becoming quite the historian, aren't you?"

Steve turned back to his notes. "Do you mind my writing about you?" His voice was steady. He wanted to know.

"Of course not," Jay answered. "Flick might raise the very roof if he knew, but not I. It's nice to keep records, Steve, and to write a little every day. I know because I do some writing myself. Straight fiction, though, nothing historical. History bores me. Much too factual."

"Then you're not afraid that people might read this someday?"

Jay laughed loudly, his voice reverberating within the close confines of the cave. "Why no, Steve," he finally said. "Who'd believe it? Take this from an old hand, Steve, it's difficult to get people to stretch their imaginations very far. They say 'it just isn't so,' and it ends there. It would be that way with this."

Jay walked to the ledge and stood there for a moment, his eyes roaming over the valley. "If I know Flick, he'll have missed me by now. Should be on his way. He's such an old fuss-budget, afraid to leave me alone a minute. . . . My, your Flame is a beauty, Steve!" he went on excitedly. "Just look at him go out there! I've never seen better action . . . as slick as light, I'd say! I do hope you've given more thought to that little trip I suggested this morning. We'd have a time, all right!" He re-entered the cave, his eyes searching Steve's.

"I won't take Flame away from the valley," Steve said, afraid for his horse. "Nothing you can do will make me."

"Oh, I know that, all right, Steve. Even if I could, I wouldn't make you do anything you didn't *want* to do. I was only suggesting that since you've had it in mind to race Flame for so long you just might take advantage of my being here and go to it."

"I was only pretending, dreaming," Steve said.

"Dreams are fine." Jay smiled. "Nothing wrong with them at all. They very often lead to the real thing."

Steve felt the heavy throbbing of his temples. He tried to look at Jay and couldn't. His notes fell to the floor and he didn't bother to pick them up.

"Oh, you *want* to race Flame, all right," Jay said. "No doubt about that. I believe what's troubling you is that you're afraid people will find out where Flame is from. That's silly, Steve. I promise you no one will learn your secret. After all, I have had a great deal of experience in that sort of thing."

Steve glanced up at Jay. He was no match for this man. It was like arguing with oneself. And he'd give so much to race Flame. If only . . .

"That's the boy, Steve," Jay said. "Just leave all the details to me. Just relax. Now what bothers me most is that Flame may not be as fast as I think he is. After all, I've been away from the races a long time, as you pointed out to me only yesterday. The horses must be very speedy these days, especially with their riders using the crouch seat."

As Steve said nothing Jay went on, "I realize you're no professional jockey but certainly you've seen them go?"

It was a question, not a statement. So there *were* some things Jay still didn't know about him! "I've watched them race a few times," he admitted.

"And Flame is faster?" Jay prodded eagerly. "After all, we wouldn't want to go to the work of getting him there and then have him *lose* the race. It would be a terrible disappointment for both of us."

Steve had no time to answer for at that moment Flick, puffing hard from his climb up the trail, entered the cave.

"What's ailing you, Jay?" Flick asked angrily. "I've never known your conduct to be worse than it's been today! I turn my back a few minutes and you're . . ."

"Now, Flick," Jay interrupted, "I just wanted to have another *private* little chat with Steve."

Flick's gaze shifted quickly to the boy and there was no lessening of the fury in his eyes. He wouldn't be having all this trouble with Jay if it hadn't been for Steve and that horse of his! He saw the notes on the floor and picked them up, his bright eyes running quickly down one page after another. Finally he put a match to them, and when the papers were afire he dropped them on the ground, stepping on the charred fragments with his small, brilliantly polished shoes.

"You shouldn't have done that, Flick," Jay admonished softly.

"Were you . . . ?" Flick sputtered and began again, "You weren't going to stand idly by and let him make use of those notes!" he shouted.

"What harm would come of it, Flick? No one would ever believe what he's written." Jay paused, and his face and voice contained only a disturbing sadness. "But the point I'm trying to make, Flick, is that you have just destroyed something which belonged to Steve and that he prized very highly. What are you going to do about it? How are you going to make amends?"

Again Flick had trouble finding his voice. "What . . . What am *I* going to do about it? You have the colossal nerve . . ."

"Ah, Flick. Be careful what you say now," Jay cautioned even more quietly. "You must remember our ironclad policy, *never to show anything but sympathy and understanding toward the people we visit.* And most important, as you very well know, is never to hurt them one bit by word or action. You've hurt Steve dreadfully. Hasn't he, Steve?"

Steve straightened in his chair. He didn't even look at the charred remains that had been his notes. It didn't matter. Neither Flick nor Jay could destroy his memory, and he would always remember. Or would they see to that too?

Jay turned back to Flick. "Well, you've hurt Steve, even if he has the graciousness not to speak of it. How do you intend to make up for what you've done?"

Flick shook his head in disgust, but a troubled look appeared in his eyes. "I know what you're suggesting," he said, "but I don't propose to do anything about it."

Jay's eyes opened wide in astonishment. "But you *must,* Flick. After all, you can't expect me to forget two such grave infractions of the rules . . . this and what happened on Mao. Actually I've done nothing to compare with either of them, as you very well know. I'm afraid I'll have to speak to Julian."

"You're being silly," Flick said hastily, but the uneasiness remained in his eyes. He turned to Steve. "I'm certain Steve doesn't want to go to the races with you," he added, a note of desperation creeping into his voice.

Jay also turned to Steve, and they silently awaited his answer.

Steve looked at them. Race Flame? Is that what he was being asked? Is that what he had to decide? Now?

"Well, Steve?" Jay asked, holding the boy's eyes. "I promised you that no one will learn your *secret.*"

Steve answered, "Flame wouldn't go with you. He'd kill you!"

"Oh, no, Steve. You're wrong," Jay said. "It's just that at this point Flame isn't being very receptive to anything we try to tell him. Isn't that right, Flick?" he asked, turning to his friend.

Flick nodded numbly, for he was looking at Steve's eyes and knew that Jay had won again. The boy really wanted to race his horse.

"You see," Jay continued, trying to make Steve understand, "Flame thinks we're evil because he heard you shout this morning when I was ... ah, when *we* were trying our little experiment. He thought I was hurting you, and now his mind is closed tight to anything but hatred of us. Right, Flick?"

Again the other's cropped head moved in sad and resigned agreement.

"Now all we need is an opportunity to reach Flame again, Steve," Jay continued. "The only possible way, of course, is for him to see you enjoying our company. It would be nice if you'd just put your arms around our shoulders. Your laughing at anything we have to say would also help. Flame will then rid himself of that mental barrier that's keeping us from reaching him. It's as simple as that. We can take the first step now by sitting down below rather than here. Come, Steve."

They went down the trail and when they were only a short distance from the valley floor they sat down. Steve saw Flame leave the band and come toward them at a run. The red stallion stopped when he saw them, his intent eyes watching every move they made.

"*Now*, Steve . . . laugh, please," Jay said, "and put your arms around our shoulders."

Steve did as Jay had requested, but his laugh was forced. It couldn't have been otherwise, for he knew that before long he and Flame would be passengers on that ship of light.

FINAL TRAINING

8

A little over an hour later Steve was sitting alone on the trail. Jay and Flick had gone moments before, and Flame was moving up the valley. Steve watched the stallion but his thoughts were of Jay's final warning.

"Of course, the big job will be yours, Steve. Do you think you can manage to get Flame out to the ship? And then once you're at the track you'll be on your own too. So please make sure you have absolute control over him. It would be terrible if he put on a bad show!"

Steve continued sitting there for many minutes, while Flame and the band moved to the most distant shadows of the valley. He wanted to go to his horse but he wasn't certain just then that his legs would bear his weight.

Finally he got to his feet, wavering a bit at first, then steadying himself enough to make his way down the trail. When he reached the valley floor he attempted a whistle but what came out wasn't loud enough to attract

Flame's attention and save him any steps. He had to go halfway up the valley before Flame saw him and stepped out of the shadows into sunlight.

Steve waited for his horse, and when Flame came to a stop beside him he put both hands up, one finding and grasping the long red mane, the other on the high withers. He steeled himself for the jump, knowing that it would take all of whatever strength he had left. He was furious at his weakness but there was no fighting it . . . or that to which he had committed himself and Flame.

There was a quivering of the stallion's muscles. Flame knew what was coming and was waiting impatiently. He sidestepped and his finely molded body moved away from Steve. Snorting through wide nostrils, Flame waited for the boy to mount. He turned his small, wedge-shaped head, his eyes surprised and puzzled at Steve's unusual clumsiness. His small ears almost touched at the tips when he pricked them forward inquisitively.

Once more Steve put his hands upon Flame. This time he jumped as high as he could, pulling at mane and back. He hung on face downward, his legs dangling. Flame whirled, and Steve's hold upon him became even more precarious. He pulled harder on the mane with one hand, the fingers of the other pressing deep into Flame's withers. Only then did the stallion come to a halt as though in sudden realization that something was terribly wrong.

Steve was successful in getting more of his weight on the off side of his horse, and finally he swung around. Flame bolted immediately, and for a while Steve made no effort to control him. He simply hung on as the stallion swept across the valley.

When Steve had brought Flame to a stop he straightened and then sat still for a moment, making certain he was all right and that he was prepared for what he had to do. After all, what had begun as the wildest of dreams was now very close to becoming a reality!

Satisfied that he was in full control of himself, he touched his horse and took him down the valley at a slow walk. Flame tried to break from it, crab-stepping and tossing his head, telling Steve in no uncertain terms that he wanted to run. But Steve did not give in to his demands. Instead, he turned Flame often, sometimes making large circles that swept them from one border of cane to the other; then again he took him in small, tight circles that made of Flame's hindquarters little more than a pivot for his tall body.

The stallion fidgeted constantly but made no attempt to break away. And that was what Steve had needed to know. He had never before asked so much of Flame at any one time.

Later he reversed the circles, keeping Flame at a walk; then he took him through figure "eights," some large, some very small and tight. Finally, allowing Flame to move into an easy lope, he made the circles and the figure "eights" again. When he had finished he was as hot as his horse, and almost as impatient.

But he did not dismount. Instead, he took Flame through the field of cane in a hard run. He kept him at that gait until they emerged from the cane and started over the stony ground near the western wall of Blue Valley. There he slowed him to a walk again and went on to the hollow near the marsh.

Flame came to a stop before the murky veil of gray and his nostrils curled. He did not like the smell of rotting vegetation any more than Steve did. But he went forward again when the pressure came from Steve's legs, his hoofs making soft, sucking sounds in the wet ground. Although he knew his way, he was very, very cautious. He had been given his head, for he was no stranger to this cloud-like world, but his eyes never left the path.

Steve glanced at the slimy wilderness of swamp ferns and high reeds on either side of them. Most of all he feared those still black pools. One false step, a slip, and he and Flame would become victims of these horrible quagmires.

Moments later they left the marsh behind, and there was a quickening of Flame's strides. He chose his path through the twisting gorge as carefully as he had done in the marsh. They went up the dry stream bed, their way strewn with rocks and boulders, the high yellow cliffs rising on either side of them. At the end of their climb the walls widened, and stretched before them was the smaller valley.

Flame broke into a run when he stepped onto dry grass again, and Steve let him go. He felt the stallion gather himself just before reaching the brook that cut the middle of the tiny valley. He knew Flame was going to jump the water rather than go through it, so he was ready when the stallion sprang from one bank to the other.

Soon after, he slowed Flame, for they were moving in a rush toward the far wall. The wall was split by many narrow chasms and Steve purposely guided Flame down one that came to a dead end. As the high, precipitous walls closed in about them, the red stallion stopped in his tracks.

He disclosed no hesitation or uneasiness when Steve asked him to back up. Instead, he let his rider become his eyes, moving his hindquarters in quick response to Steve's touches. And finally he was free of the narrow, twisting chasm.

Steve felt no great elation at Flame's easy and prompt obedience to his requests. The test of final, complete control over Flame was yet to come.

He rode Flame alongside the wall, and then turned him into the chasm that led to the sea entrance. Soon he could hear the dull thud of waves beating against the outer wall. He stopped Flame at the end of the chasm and dismounted.

"Come on, boy," he said, entering the high cave. There was no need to look back, for he heard Flame's hoofbeats behind him.

He hurried through the large cave, having no trouble making his way in the dim, gray light. Flame followed him with equal ease for he, too, had been there many times. At last they entered the great chamber, and the winds from the sea whipped about them. The crash of waves outside was thunderous as was the rush of water in the canal. The motor launch rocked against the wooden piles. It was here, Steve knew, that the final test of his control over Flame would come.

The stallion stopped just within the chamber. Steve

glanced back at him, and then went to the launch. He hauled out the wide planks that were used in sliding barrels and heavy boxes onto the sunken deck and then called to his horse, "Come on, boy!"

Flame came quickly, showing no fear or hesitation until Steve stepped aboard the launch and continued calling him. Then he stopped, his eyes on the boy, and backed away, only to come forward again. He snorted and pawed the sand, sending it flying. He carried on for many minutes without setting hoof on the planks. He knew what he was being asked to do.

Steve sat down in the boat, talking to Flame, and waiting. His task would take a long time, if he succeeded in it at all. Whenever Flame moved away from the launch Steve called to him again. The stallion's eyes were bright in his bewilderment, and once he ran out of the chamber. Steve stayed in the boat and finally Flame returned to plunge about the sandy floor, his snorts softening the crash of waves outside.

"We're not going anywhere," Steve told him. "I just want to see if you'll do it."

It was a long while before Flame even consented to lower his small head to smell the wooden planks. He walked up and down the canal, sniffing the hull of the launch. Then he turned abruptly away and began plunging about the chamber once more. Finally he settled down but stood in a far corner, waiting patiently for Steve to return to Blue Valley.

After a half-hour had passed Flame lost his patience. As he snorted and came forward, Steve rose and stood close to the planks. "Come, Flame," he said softly, "and then we'll go back."

Flame angrily tossed his head and rose high on his hind legs, almost touching the top of the chamber. When he came down he stood still, watching Steve and listening to him. He put one hoof on a plank, then quickly took it off. He tried the other hoof and this one remained planted on the plank. A few seconds more and the second hoof had joined it. And thus he stood, making no sound, two hind feet on sand, two forefeet on wood. He listened to the rhythm of the boy's voice and inched forward carefully. Then he stopped again, undecided.

When he finally went down the planks, it was with an abruptness that shook the boat. There was a lurching of his great body, the hard thud of all four hoofs on wood planking, and then a restless shifting of his weight once he was aboard.

Fortunately the *Sea Queen* was a sturdy vessel and she easily withstood the stallion's constant movement. Steve stayed close to Flame's head, talking to him, comforting him. The sides of the launch were not very high, and Flame could have jumped onto the sandy floor. But he didn't. He knew Steve wanted him in the boat and for the moment he was willing to stay there. He had no room to turn, he could hardly move. Finally he quieted and looked inquisitively at the wheel and the glistening brass objects behind Steve.

Steve backed up to the wheel then and Flame, taking a cautious step forward, followed. Now very curious and unafraid, he thrust his small head beneath the wooden overhang. Seeing this, Steve realized that he would be able to take Flame in the launch, but that it would be a hazardous trip for the first few hundred yards. He'd have all he could do to guide the boat safely through the submerged coral rock, much less have time to watch his horse.

Was he actually considering taking Flame from Azul Island? Even if they were successful in reaching Cuba, what about the still greater risks they'd be taking at the track? Jay knew nothing of the rules and regulations governing the running of a race of this magnitude, and neither did he! What would he say when the officials asked him where he and his horse were from? *The Windward Islands of the Caribbean Sea?* Would that satisfy them? Would they accept such a vague answer and allow him to race Flame? Just because the poster had said that the International Race was open to the world? Of course not! In the end they'd make him divulge everything and Flame might even be taken from him!

"Come on, Flame," he said. "We're going back *to stay.*" He stepped out of the launch and his horse followed him eagerly, glad to be returning to Blue Valley.

The Unleashing

9

Steve moved away from the stove where he had been cooking his evening meal. Flame and the mares were drinking at the pool below. For a long while Steve stood watching them, the skin drawn tight on his angular face. He wasn't going to race Flame at the risk of losing him! He didn't care what he had told Jay. He had changed his mind . . . and Jay couldn't make him do anything he didn't *want* to do. Hadn't Jay said so, time and time again?

He went back to the stove and put his dinner on a plate. But when he sat down, he found he was toying with his food. Was his appetite never coming back? Or was it simply that whatever he cooked was tasteless compared to Pitch's meals?

Long after night had fallen, he kept trying to convince himself that he had made up his mind, that he had no intention of taking Flame to Cuba. Actually it was this that was absorbing him, leaving no room for appetite or sleep.

When the first streaks of dawn appeared in the sky, Steve turned face downward on his cot. Closing his eyes, he sought the rest that had evaded him throughout the night. Once more he tried to rid his mind of every thought but sleep. He forced himself to see only a heavy black curtain. He concentrated on the blackness, and waited for sleep to come. But heavy hands seemed to part his mental curtain and divulge all that lay behind, all that had kept him awake for so many hours. He fought to keep the curtain closed, to see only the blackness. His head and pillow were wet and clammy with sweat, yet he continued fighting and refused to give up. But it was a losing battle. The hands were winning; he felt their pull. Then the curtain opened and his mind began racing again. He decided to get up. As tired as he was he couldn't fight any longer.

He felt the hands on his shoulders, shaking him gently . . . only these hands were real, as was the voice.

"Steve, are you awake?" Jay asked.

As Steve turned over, he could see Jay's eyes glowing in the semi-darkness of the cave.

"I'm sorry that I've awakened you so early, Steve, but I couldn't wait any longer to tell you what I've learned!"

Jay sat down on the cot, but got up again quickly. "I'm a little too excited to sit still, I guess. I've found a wonderful place to land, Steve. Actually it's much closer to Cuba than I thought we dared go. Even Flick seems satisfied that we won't be seen."

Jay chuckled before adding, "Flick thought I meant to bring the ship down between Cuba and Florida. Really, he doesn't give me credit for having any sense at all, sometimes. As though I weren't well aware of the tourist traffic there."

Jay moved past the cot, pacing the cave restlessly. "I feel just like a race horse going to the post. Really I do, Steve. Planning this trip of ours is the most exciting thing I've done in a long, long time. But it's only natural, I suppose, when I think that we're working this out *together*. Nothing like it has ever happened before to *any* of us." He stopped abruptly and his eyes glowed less brightly. "Oh, my, if Julian ever hears of this! But he won't. Flick wouldn't dare tell him."

Jay began pacing again, then stopped and sat down beside Steve. "I can see I've startled you by coming so early. You must have been sound asleep. Really, Steve, I *am* sorry, but you'll understand my impatience when I tell you the rest."

He rose and went to the ledge, talking all the while. "Quite close to Cuba is a small group of islands. We'll come in off the most eastern of the group. Using your launch you won't have any trouble reaching a small fishing village on the Cuban coast. This village is about fifty miles, I'd say, from Havana and the track. Really, Steve, it's going to be much easier than we thought. I'm sure we won't be seen coming in, and your trip to shore with Flame will be a very short one. We can only bring our ship down at sea, you know. It couldn't have worked out better. Even Flick has raised no objections."

Jay retraced his steps and stood in front of Steve. "You're not saying much, Steve." He laughed. "But then I haven't given you much of a chance, have I? Aren't you pleased with what I've learned?"

Only then did Steve remove his gaze from Jay's

eyes. He saw what looked like a rope in the man's hand. Jay was twirling it in his excitement and it too glowed in the semi-darkness. Jay must have noticed his interest for suddenly it was offered to him and he held it in his own hands. Only it wasn't a rope at all. It was as soft as flesh and just as pliant. It had no weight and yet there was a good deal of it, fashioned in the shape of a hack-amore, complete with reins. It had no color at all and yet contained the most brilliant of all colors. The fibers pulsated beneath his fingers, seemingly alive and warm. He was not frightened. Instead he held it close, looking at the long golden tassels that hung from it.

"That's my race offering, Steve," Jay said quietly. "I figured you'd need some kind of a headpiece in guiding Flame. I realize you use nothing of the kind here, but it will be different at the track. Besides, it would look very strange to have you out there with nothing on him at all, no bridle or saddle. I don't suppose they'll require you to use a saddle, but they'll insist upon your having some obvious control over your horse's head. They'd never believe you if you said you needed nothing at all. And I think you'll need the hackamore, Steve. Really I do. I'm sure Flame won't mind wearing it. He'll hardly know it's on. Try it today."

Steve looked up at him. "We're not going," he said quietly.

For the first time wrinkles appeared in Jay's high brow, and the light suddenly was gone from his eyes. He looked at Steve a long while, and then sat down beside him.

"You've changed your mind then?" he asked.

Steve nodded.

"All right, Steve, if that's the way you think you want it. But you really don't, you know. You're very anxious to race Flame."

With that he got up again and stood before Steve, watching him, waiting for him to speak. And when the boy remained silent, he said, "Of course I'm disappointed. But above all, Steve, I don't want you feeling sorry later on that you missed this chance. Promise me that, won't you?"

Still Steve said nothing.

"I know you're worried about a lot of things, Steve, and I'm sorry that I can't help you more. It's impossible for me to reassure you that Flame will win the race. What Flame does on the track is strictly up to you and him. I've told you before that your part in all this is much more difficult than mine. But that's the chance you must take. I can't help you there."

Steve said, "It's not what might happen during the race that has made me change my mind."

"It isn't?" Jay was surprised. "I thought for sure . . ." He paused, looking more intently into the boy's eyes. Then he said, "But I promised you that no one will learn of your secret valley, Steve. It just won't be possible for anyone to see you and Flame travel between this island and Cuba. You have my word that I've gotten away with much more than this during my travels."

Steve turned away. "I'm sure you have," he answered. "But I don't think you have any idea of what I'll be up against at the track. The officials will want to know where we're from. What will I tell them? And what will they do when they're not satisfied with my answer? They might even take Flame from me, thinking perhaps that I've stolen him!"

The frown returned to Jay's face. "I don't believe they would do that, Steve. But I never really considered *details* like that. I thought you'd just go and race, and then return to the ship. I can understand your concern now, but I'm sure something can be worked out. Let's see. . . ."

Steve interrupted before Jay could continue. "I'm certain there are many rules governing the running of a race such as this. We don't just . . ."

"But you said it was *Open to the World,* Steve," Jay insisted. "Doesn't that mean what it says? If it's an open race, it's open to any horse in the world which may want to race in it. You have every legal right to race Flame. You can demand it!"

Jay was shaking his head angrily, and his blue-black hair fell down over his forehead, making him look very funny. The whole thing was so absurd that Steve laughed. Was he actually in this cave in a lost valley, listening to a man from another world remind him of his legal rights?

"Don't laugh, Steve," Jay said. "You have every right to demand that you be allowed to race Flame. After all, if you can't believe what you read here on Earth, why . . ."

Steve interrupted again. "But I *still* have to answer their questions. And they'll ask where we're from."

"You and Flame are from this world, aren't you?" Jay demanded. "That's all that is necessary to tell them."

Steve made no reply. Instead he looked around

him, finding familiar objects . . . the stove, Pitch's pipes and can of tea, the trunks and boxes, anything at all to help him keep his mental balance.

Jay lapsed into a moment of thoughtful silence, then his hand descended roughly on Steve's shoulder. "I've got it, Steve. I know exactly what we can do." Swinging around, he sat down on the cot.

"Flick's been pretty insistent that we just drop you and Flame off near Cuba while I join you later for the race itself. But I think that when I tell him of your grave concern for Flame's safety he might be convinced that it's necessary for me to remain with you. After all, it's pretty important to us too that you don't run into any trouble with the officials. We mustn't start a lot of talk.

"Now near this fishing village I mentioned there are several homes that are closed tight," Jay continued. "I'm certain they're available for rental, and one has a small stable behind it."

"How do you know all this?" Steve asked.

"I told you I found out early last night, Steve," Jay answered impatiently. "Flick was agreeable to my taking the cruiser and doing a little reconnaissance. It took only a few minutes. It'll be nothing at all in the big ship. Whiff! . . . and we're there."

Steve's head reeled. Only a few minutes . . . with Cuba almost two thousand miles away! Jay was going on, unmindful of the impact of his words upon Steve.

"I'll stay with Flame while you go to Havana and find out if this race is open to the world or isn't. If it is, you return for Flame and race him. If it isn't, we bring you back here. It's all very simple, and I can't see that anything can go wrong."

Steve rose from the cot. "But how will we get him to Havana? He can't walk fifty miles and then race."

"Of course not, Steve. There you go, bothering yourself with details again! We'll hire a truck. I'm sure there must be a number available in the village. And don't say that we don't have any Cuban money. I'll attend to that. Really, Steve, in some ways you're so much like Flick. You don't give me any credit for . . ."

Jay stopped, and then added apologetically, "I didn't mean that the way it sounded, Steve. I'm very fond of you, just as I am of Flick. But I wish you would let me attend to a *few* things. I've really been very busy, much more so than you may think. After I got back from Cuba I went right to work on this hackamore, and I still have plenty to do. I must make a blanket for Flame, Steve. I won't have him uncovered while he's hot."

Jumping nimbly to his feet, Jay patted the boy's shoulder. "You relax now, Steve, and leave all the details to me. You'll have plenty to do just seeing to it that Flame runs the best race he can. Oh, I do hope he doesn't let us down!"

Jay started for the ledge, stopped and said, "We'll leave *tomorrow at sunset,* Steve. It's very important that you be not a minute late. We'll glow a bit coming in even though it is only a skip. Don't fail me now."

After Jay had gone Steve looked at the living, fibrous tissue of the strange hackamore. His fingers closed over it and he felt its warmth, the same warmth and trust Jay and Flick conveyed to him whenever they were near. Somehow he knew it had taken their place. He hoped they would let him keep it always.

He left the cave then, knowing what he had to do. He whistled to Flame before going down the trail, and the stallion was there to meet him when he reached the valley floor.

For a moment he let Flame smell the bitless bridle. Flame, nuzzling the long tassels of sheer thread, showed no fear of it.

When Steve slipped the bridle on him the fibers seemed to shorten, causing the bridle to fit snugly about Flame's small head. But the golden tassels, hanging below and on either side of his large nostrils, remained their original length. Steve led Flame back to the trail and, after mounting, drew up the reins.

He sat quietly on Flame's back, and the stallion made no move. Then Steve leaned forward, whispering. He looked down the valley at the long stretch before them. He waited and Flame waited too. Both were tense and eager to go. Eyes were straight ahead. Flame's ears were pricked. The waiting became harder but neither moved. Muscles were strained almost to the breaking point. Then, just as the first rays of the morning sun struck the dome of Azul Island, came the unleashing, the end of waiting.

"Go!" called Steve, and on either side of them raced the horses of the world.

THE ROOM

10

Sunset the following day came swiftly to Steve Duncan, and now he stood beside his horse in the great sea chamber. He looked at the soft flow of water in the narrow canal as it rocked the launch quietly against the aged wooden piles. Even the sea was encouraging him to leave, for most days the canal was white with salty foam from great waves crashing against the outer wall before finding their way inside. How often he and Pitch had awaited just such a calm sea as this before undertaking the perilous passage through the coral rock!

Steve whispered to his horse but made no effort to lead him down the wide planks. Flame wore his hackamore and the long tassels seemed alive when he tossed his head, snorting at the launch. If it had not been for the hackamore, Steve might have believed that Jay and Flick had never been, that he could not be leaving Azul Island with Flame! He had not seen Jay since the early morning visit of the day before.

It was almost sunset. They had better be on their

way quickly and yet . . . Steve did not move and the seconds passed, long seconds filled with dread and doubts and yet wonderful dreams as well. He felt the lines of the bitless bridle contract in the palms of his perspiring hands, becoming as light as the sheerest thread yet heavy in their lifelike throbbing.

He knew what he was about to do, and that he had no *earthly* right to be doing it. Soon he and Flame would be passengers aboard that ship from outer space. It was all so fantastic, so incredible . . . but all so true. As true and real as his standing there beside Flame. And he was about to go of his own free will. That too was true.

"Come, Flame," he said.

The red stallion raised his forefeet to the planks, took another step and then stood still, his legs rigid.

Steve waited, talking to him all the while. He held the lines taut but did not pull, and neither did Flame. The daylight coming through the low sea hole was fading, but Steve did not want to open the wide doors above the hole until Flame was aboard the launch, his head turned away from the outer world. He must not become frightened by what he saw.

Steve's voice became edgy in his anxiety over the growing darkness. He was late now, for Jay had said that it was most important to be at the ship by sunset. He began to turn Flame's head one way and then the other, trying to get him to shift his balance, to move his forelegs.

"Come, Flame," he repeated urgently.

The long, straight legs moved a little, the small head bent down, sniffing the boards. The chamber grew darker. Desperately Steve pulled on the lines. What if they didn't leave after all! He realized then how much he really wanted to go with Jay and Flick.

Flame raised his head at Steve's urgent pull on the lines. His large eyes met the boy's curiously, wanting to know just how much was expected of him.

"You've done this before, Flame," Steve pleaded.

The stallion bent his head once more, sniffing the boards, his nostrils blown wide.

Steve turned Flame's head from one side to the other. Suddenly the horse's forelegs shifted, and there was a great lurching of his body. The sound of his hoofs on the boards thudded hollowly as he followed Steve onto the launch.

The first step had been taken! Steve stood still for a moment, stroking his horse, quieting him. Then he tied the lines to the gunwale, although he knew that nothing would hold Flame if he really wanted to get away. He continued talking while he went behind Flame to the stern; there he slid open the wooden doors to the sea.

A fresh evening breeze swept into the chamber with the increased light. But Steve felt utter dismay when he saw how low the sun had descended. Another moment and it would be gone!

Suddenly Flame shifted his weight, and the launch rocked as he sought to turn his head, to see what lay behind him.

Steve hurried to Flame, but he could not stay there long. He had no time. For him, a dangerous game of chance had begun, and there was no turning back, now or ever. He switched on the ignition, and the engine caught with a sudden roar made louder by the close confines of the chamber. The sound startled Flame and Steve touched him lightly, trying to comfort him. At the same time he had the launch moving, backing slowly out of the chamber.

As the boat slid along the canal, Flame tore the lines loose from the gunwale. Steve grabbed them, keeping his horse from rearing as the launch swept through the exit.

They rose with the swells of the sea, and Flame screamed shrilly. But there was not much else he could do, with open water on either side of him.

Steve continued talking to his horse, trying to reassure him that everything was all right. He would have liked to close the doors of the sea chamber, but without Pitch's help it was impossible. That someone might discover the entrance to Azul Island during his absence was another hazard in the dangerous game he was playing.

Flame looked all around, constantly screaming while the launch backed farther away from the sheer wall of stone. Suddenly Steve turned the wheel and the boat slid between two pieces of rock whose tips just broke the surface. Then the launch went forward, its prow pointed toward the open sea.

The sun had set, and only the brilliant afterglow remained. Carefully and slowly, Steve guided the launch through the coral reef.

Behind him he heard the dull thud of Flame's pawing. He continued talking to the stallion, soothing him with words while his eyes and thoughts were momentarily elsewhere. Then the pawing stopped, and he heard the quick shifting of hoofs. He felt Flame's hot breath on his neck, but he couldn't turn to him, couldn't take his eyes off the narrow channel ahead. Nor could he reach back and touch Flame, for both hands were needed on the wheel. So he stood there quietly and terribly concerned, becoming alarmed for himself and his horse, and all that lay beyond.

The white patch he sought lay a few hundred yards past the last of the coral reefs. It rose gracefully with the giant swells but remained always in the same spot, as if it were anchored to the depths of the Caribbean.

By this time the brilliance of the heavens had faded and the sky was a pale, murky red. As Steve neared the patch it too changed color, becoming phosphorescent in the twilight of early evening. He knew that he had arrived much too late, but there was no turning back. He could not come again another day ... he would not have had the courage to return. For now, with the patch directly before him, he felt all the fears he had successfully imprisoned seeking release. He tried to quell his mounting dread. He repeated everything he had told himself so many times. He must accept Jay and Flick and their world. He must be confident and trusting. He must believe in them.

"I have nothing to fear except what I've learned to fear in this world," he said aloud.

But his spoken words rang with insincerity. Now, nothing he could say could crush the doubts, the suspicions and fears which rose within him. His hands turned the wheel, seeking to take the launch away from the patch. He would return to Blue Valley and all that he knew to be standard and normal and sane.

The wheel turned easily but the boat did not

respond to the change in course. Its prow cut the waters directly ahead, drawing closer and closer to the luminous patch. Even when Steve reversed the propeller there was no slackening of their forward speed!

He knew then that the launch was no longer under *his* control. He turned to Flame for comfort, but the stallion held his head high, his bright eyes staring beyond. No sound came from him, and Steve turned to look with him at the area above the patch, which was now bathed in a golden light that grew in size and brilliance. The waters below it turned from a deep, dark blue to a bubbling silver gray. The swells disappeared, leaving the sea flat.

The prow of the boat pierced the veiled, golden shroud and then came to an abrupt stop, throwing Steve and Flame forward. Before their eyes the bow rose and they stumbled backward, their simultaneous cries shattering the silent evening. Then they too were enveloped by the light.

Steve felt the wooden deck rise beneath his feet, yet he could not see the launch or Flame or anything else. His keenest sense was that of great empty spaces all around him, and he stared into the vastness seeing nothing at all, not even light or darkness. And yet, strangely enough, all dread and fear had left him.

From close beside him Jay said, "Get out, Steve. You're here at last."

"I am?" he asked into the nothing, his voice echoing and re-echoing in the vast, empty void.

"Of course," Jay said, impatient now. "I'm having such a time with Flick because you're late. He's afraid we'll be seen and now he doesn't want to go at all."

Steve felt Jay's hands on his arm but he could not see him. He knew he was being guided hurriedly off the launch because he went up what he knew were the planks leading from the deck. Behind him came Flame. But he could not hear the stallion's hoofs any more than he could his own footsteps.

"Careful, Steve," Jay cautioned. "Watch your step. We're getting off now."

Steve thought it ridiculous to be told to watch his step when he could see nothing but those murky, endless spaces of . . . Of what? He couldn't decide. But they were there all the same.

He stepped from that void into a great room. Jay, whom he could now see, went over to the stallion and straightened the brow band of the hackamore.

"I do wish you had started earlier, Steve," he said gravely without taking his eyes off Flame. "I'm not sure what's going to happen now. Flick's in a very nervous state."

Steve glanced around the room in which they stood.

"You won't find him here," Jay said. "He went to the chart room to check the screen."

It wasn't important to Steve where Flick was. He took hold of the lines of the hackamore, grasping them tightly for support, while he took another look around the room.

The walls were hung with great tapestries which changed color constantly before his eyes, becoming shades he recognized and still others that no one in this world had ever seen before. It was their movement that caused him to tremble suddenly. They seemed to be alive and breathing! They all billowed together and glowed in a new and fiery brilliance. He stared at them, feeling their resentment at his very presence.

Jay noted the alarm in Steve's eyes and said kindly, "Don't let them bother you. They're disturbed easily but soon get over it." Then, smiling, "Of course you're very new to them," he added.

"Then they are real," Steve said. *"They're alive."*

"In a way, Steve. In the same way everything is alive in one form or another. Nothing is ever really dead, you know."

There was neither depth nor height to the room, neither length nor width. Steve felt that he could walk forever without ever reaching those living walls, that the harder he tried the farther back they would move. Suddenly their colors changed again. They were no longer an angry red but were billowing in soft, somber tones. Yet they continued to move, breathing lightly as if at rest in their final acceptance of him.

"See, Steve," Jay said. "They've settled down again, just as I said they would." He placed an arm around the boy's shoulders. "Let's have a seat now and decide on the best way to handle Flick."

Steve let Jay guide him forward. There seemed to be a floor of soft metal beneath his feet, so pliable that it yielded with every step he took.

He stopped in his tracks once, turning his head to see where Flame was. The stallion was still standing where Jay had left him, his red coat shining brighter than ever against the background of colorless, empty space from which they had emerged. But it was not empty space, Steve reminded himself. The launch had to be there, somewhere.

Flame's head was held high, his neck arched in a manner that he seldom maintained for very long. Steve noticed that the lines of the hackamore hung tautly to the floor, as though held by the molten metal itself.

"Let him be, Steve," Jay said. "It's the easiest way of handling him now. We don't want him upset, and it's only for a little while. He's resting comfortably. Sit down, please."

There were no chairs, no furniture in this endless room. Yet Jay gently pushed him down and Steve felt a support of some sort beneath him. Whatever it was, it hugged him close, molding itself to his figure even when he moved his arms and legs. Never before had he sat so comfortably or been so relaxed, so completely at ease.

"That's it, Steve," Jay said approvingly, "just take it nice and easy. Let me figure out the best way of handling Flick. Of course he's absolutely right about the possibility of our being seen when we don't have the setting sun as a backdrop for our landing."

He paused, turning his disturbed eyes upon Steve. "In a night sky this ship is about as concealable as a fireball. We haven't been able to do much about that, Steve, not yet. No more than we can get rid of those gases that lie upon the water after we do arrive. They're apt to betray our location to anyone who knows the score, as you found out for yourself.

"But getting back to our traveling at night. I say we ought to take a chance on it, don't you, Steve? What can your people think we are but a falling star or, at most, a meteor, as you did. *Whisk,* we're down and away in the launch. *Whisk,* Flick and the ship are back here. Nothing to it, really, if I can just get old Flick to think along those lines."

Jay recrossed his legs and thoughtfully rubbed his smooth chin. Steve watched him, trying hard to concentrate on what Jay was saying. But to have this man sitting so comfortably beside him with no visible support was at that moment more astounding than anything else. He looked down at his own legs, one on the floor, the other outstretched. What was supporting *him*?

Suddenly Flick appeared in front of the nearest wall, and Jay called out to him, "Well, Flick, I guess you're satisfied that we can go now, aren't you?"

"Not in the least," the other answered, nodding to Steve and then sitting down beside him. "The screen shows plenty of lights there. We haven't a chance of landing without being seen."

"So what?" Jay asked defiantly. "You'll be back here before they know what it's all about."

Flick shook his head. "It'll cause talk, though, and that we must avoid. You know the rules, Jay, as well as I do, and we'd be taking a very unnecessary risk going at this hour."

Jay glared at him. "Unnecessary to you but not to us," he bellowed. "After all, Flick, you *promised.*"

"I promised a good many things that I never should have," Flick returned gravely. "However, that can't be helped now, and I mean to go through with it but not at the expense of the ship's being seen. You and Steve will just have to put off going until tomorrow."

"I don't know if Steve would come back," Jay said

sullenly. "After all, this is a pretty unusual thing for him to be doing."

Steve said nothing. He remembered how he had tried to steer the launch off course just before reaching the patch, how at the last moment he had sought the normalcy of his own world. Yet now he was in this ship, startled and astounded by all he saw but seated quietly, waiting for Jay and Flick to decide what to do because he had arrived late. But would he have the courage to return tomorrow?

Jay rose to his feet and began pacing the great room. Finally he stopped in front of Flick and said, "We'd better have Steve spend the night with us."

Flick jumped to his feet. *"Jay!"* he said sharply. "Remaining on the ship is out of the question. Why . . ."

He stopped abruptly and wheeled around, facing the far wall. Steve's gaze shifted with Flick's, and he saw the tapestries billowing as if a great wind had swept the room. Somehow he knew that they were upset by the noise in the room and by the very suggestion that he should spend the night there. Without saying a word he got to his feet.

"Now, Steve," Jay said softly. "Don't *you* go getting upset, too. It's bad enough to have Flick raging around here without your doing it as well. Sit down, please."

After Steve was seated again, Jay turned to Flick. "If you won't agree to his spending the night, it must be now or never, Flick."

"I'm afraid it must be *never* then," Flick answered, matching Jay's defiance.

"You'd break a promise?"

"I would when it involves the disturbance and talk

we'd create by moving the ship at night," Flick answered more calmly. "After all, Jay, you know as well as I do that the little glimpse these people have had recently of our *cruisers* have been trouble enough. If we're not careful we won't be allowed to visit Earth any more."

"Oh, pshaw," Jay said. "The cruisers couldn't upset anyone."

"If that's the way you feel, why don't you take ours then?" Flick suggested reasonably. "You're perfectly right . . . probably no one will even see you."

"It would be much too small and uncomfortable with Flame in it," Jay answered after a moment's thought.

Flick smiled critically. "So now you're thinking of the few discomforts you may have to endure while helping Steve to race his horse. My, Jay, you are the one, aren't you?"

Jay shifted uneasily and avoided looking at Steve when he said, "One doesn't like to be cramped."

"Of course not," Flick answered, still smiling. "Let's not suffer any discomforts while helping our fellow man."

"You know we wouldn't have room to move even the slightest bit," Jay said sheepishly.

"Terrible," Flick agreed sadly. "And for just those *few* minutes it would take to get there!"

"Steve wouldn't like to go that way at all!" Jay returned, a little defiantly.

"Wouldn't you, Steve?" Flick asked, turning to the boy.

Steve said, "I don't care how we go. Flame didn't have room to move in the launch, either."

Flick chuckled. "See, Jay? I hope you'll learn something from all this. In fact, you might change quite a bit before you're through with Steve and Flame."

"All right," Jay said finally, "if that's the only way you'll have it. But it's not going to be very comfortable." He got to his feet. "Come on, Steve," he added resignedly.

"Oh, just one thing more," Flick said, enjoying his moment of triumph. "You must promise not to take any unnecessary chances when you're with . . . ah . . . with other people."

"I promise," Jay said angrily. "Of course I promise."

"And if I send for you, you'll come straight back whether the race has been run or not?" Flick asked, more serious now.

"Of course!" Jay screamed at the top of his voice. "Anything else, Flick? Anything else?"

At Jay's loud words, Steve saw the hanging tapestries boil into a turmoil of seething, angry crimson again. Instinctively his footsteps quickened to catch up with Jay's.

Together they went toward the great red stallion, who stood silently awaiting them.

AND A STAR TO GUIDE HER BY

11

Jay turned Flame's head to one side so the stallion could see Steve. "Now take him inside," he said quietly.

The lines of the hackamore were placed in Steve's hands and he felt the heat of Flame's blood flowing through them. Stepping back into the colorless veil from which he had entered the room, he was conscious once more of the sudden brightness that burned his eyes. Then it was gone and there was neither light nor darkness, only a deep sense of vast, empty space all around him. He could see nothing, no part of himself or Flame or Jay.

"Careful of that tank, Steve!" Jay said impatiently.

Steve stopped in his tracks and waited.

"What's wrong?" Jay asked more kindly.

From somewhere behind them Flick said scornfully, "You've forgotten again that Steve can't see a thing in this port, Jay."

For a moment heavy silence filled the vastness, and

then Jay said, "Sorry, Steve. Details again, at which I've admitted my shortcomings."

Steve felt Jay's hand on his arm, guiding him to the left. He was not certain but he thought he saw a faint glow just ahead. He looked harder, wanting to *see*.

Jay mumbled something about untrained eyes, and Flick asked gravely, "Where do you think we'd be if their eyes *were* trained?"

"Not here, sure enough," Jay answered.

"Then don't ever forget it again. Now I'll check the screen once more. Don't leave until I get back."

Steve continued looking at the shimmering glow. Was it not growing? A few moments more and his eyes began to burn fiercely and he had to turn away.

Jay said, "I guess we might as well get aboard, Steve, although I don't like the idea of spending any more time than necessary in there. However, Flick should be back any second now. Come, follow me."

Steve didn't move, for Jay's hand had left his shoulder. "Where?" he asked.

"Why, right here, of course," and once more Jay's hand was on his arm.

Steve took a step forward, at the same time trying desperately to pierce the void. It was as though he were walking with closed eyelids, actually seeing nothing but conscious of a whole world about him.

"Lower Flame's head a little, Steve. Unfortunately this door wasn't meant for anyone but ourselves and we're a small race, as you know. However, if I raise this top partition he'll be able to make it. Sometimes we do have to carry a bit of cargo in these cruisers . . .

never very comfortably though," Jay added with a twinge of regret.

Steve heard a soft whirring noise. Once again he concentrated on the area directly before him. *It* had to be there, somewhere.

For what seemed a long while he saw nothing, then the small glow appeared again, spreading more rapidly than before. His eyes began to burn but he refused to turn away this time. And he saw it was no glow at all but a thin, liquid mass. It was an elongated bubble, growing brighter and larger, glistening in his eyes and setting them afire. Then suddenly it seemed to burst in his face and he turned away quickly to avoid its spitting, liquid fingers.

Nothing touched him. Nothing burned except his eyes, and he wondered if he would ever be able to see again. Then he heard Jay's voice.

"There, Steve, Flame should be able to get through now. Just lower his head a bit more."

Steve dropped his right hand, feeling the weight of Flame's head at the end of the lines. Didn't Jay know that for a few seconds he had actually *seen* the cruiser?

"Come, Steve. I'm anxious to be off the second Flick returns. We've wasted enough time already."

Steve was led forward and when they came to a stop he knew they were inside the cruiser.

"I'll take Flame now," Jay said. "My, this is going to be a most uncomfortable trip!"

The lines were removed from Steve's hand, but Jay did not take Flame away. Instead, Steve heard the man's soft, birdlike mutterings. Finally Jay said, "There, he's resting again. It'll be safest during the trip."

And from outside came Flick's voice, "All right, Jay.

There are no lights except in the village. Be sure to land to the east of it."

"Of course," Jay answered bitterly. "I had no intention of landing anywhere else. Really, Flick . . ." He stopped without finishing his sentence, and then said to Steve, "Sit down, but move more to your right, please, so I'll have a *little* room for my legs. That's it."

"Remember what I said about taking no unnecessary chances," Flick warned.

"Of course," Jay said. "Don't worry so, Flick."

Flick grunted. "You're all set then?"

"As set as we'll ever be in this thing," Jay muttered. "At least we don't have to take Steve's launch now. That's something to be thankful for."

Steve heard the soft whirring noise again and knew the cruiser's door was being closed. Any moment now and they'd be off! His heart pounded at the thought. One hand left his side, reaching high and groping until it found Flame."

The fear within him said, *"Here you go, never to return."*

"Don't be silly," he answered. "They're my friends."

"You'll never see your real friends again. Do you think any of your friends would change places with you? Of course not!"

"They would if they were here, if they had looked into Jay's and Flick's eyes."

"What a child you are to believe that."

Steve felt the hot blood rushing through his body. "I'm no child," he said defiantly. "I'm big, as big as anyone could be because of their help. I'm the luckiest fellow in this world! I'm not afraid!"

The cruiser moved.

There was no blinding glare of atomic or hydrogen power, no great roar for which Steve had prepared himself. He was aware at first only of rocking gently backwards in his seat and of the swaying of Flame's great body beneath his hand. Then there was no movement at all. Nothing but deathly silence. No hum of powerful engines, no darkness, no light. Everything was the same as before, and yet he knew they were on their way.

Jay said, "You're not even looking, Steve. I thought you'd like to see where we're going."

"But there's nothing to see," Steve protested.

Jay chuckled. "There is, if you'll just turn your head and look out the window."

Steve turned quickly and looked out into a night sky studded with multitude upon multitude of stars. They were very bright and there were many more than he had ever seen before. But otherwise he could have been back in Blue Valley looking up at the heavens.

He felt no sense of flight and yet, he figured, they must be traveling at frightening speed to go almost two thousand miles in a matter of a few minutes. He steeled himself to peer below . . . as one would have done from a very precarious height with no secure hold. Yet there was nothing to be seen below.

"Where are we?" he asked.

Jay laughed again. "Straight up," he said. "We literally hop, just as I told you. Up and then down. Faster that way and less chance to be seen, scarcely any friction at all. We learned long ago not to cruise below. Your people always mistake us for something else."

"And *your* people, Jay, where are they?" Steve

asked, his eyes fixed once more on the splendor and brilliance of the sky. "Is Alula one of those?"

"Oh, no, Steve. We're much further beyond. What you see is nothing. You've no idea what lies beyond."

"No . . . no, I haven't," Steve said, patting Flame.

"This is only your galaxy," Jay went on, "nine planets and something like a hundred thousand million stars. Flick would know the exact figures. I'm always a little hazy on things like that."

"Is there other life on our planets?"

"Life? I told you once before that nothing is ever really dead, Steve."

"But people, Jay . . . are there other people?"

"*People?* No, no people, Steve. You have to go beyond for that." Jay moved his legs, brushing against Steve's. "Sorry," he said. "I'm trying to get rid of a bad cramp. If you'd just move your right leg a bit more. There, that's better. Oh, this is the worst kind of discomfort!"

Steve said nothing, and Jay added, "But thank goodness we're just about there."

Silence again closed upon them, silence and always the stars, but now Steve was aware of movement for the first time since take-off. Not the cruiser's movement, but the quick shifting of the heavens. The stars began to slip by, slowly at first and then more rapidly until they were no longer stars but long, fiery tails streaming through the night sky.

Steve did not need to be told that the cruiser was descending.

Jay said with relief, "Another few seconds now, Steve. Sit back, please."

But Steve couldn't sit back, for the stars were gone.

In their place was his world, the sea and the land beyond. Not just the tiny specks he knew must be the islands of the Greater Antilles but the great, bulging masses of North and South America as well.

Then, as with the stars, the two continents were gone. Only the sea remained and the one small island that grew rapidly before his eyes. Still and silent it awaited them, a land of papier-mâché mountains and heavier-than-night depths.

Suddenly the land and sea became alive. Distant lights that were not stars twinkled in cities and scattered villages. Cars moved across a great plain. A boat pushed its prow into the sea, churning white the dark waters before it while the smoke from its lone stack billowed gray in the night sky.

There was a quickening blur before Steve's eyes and then he saw nothing. Startled, he drew back, afraid that they were about to crash into the earth. He felt the forward swaying of his body, then a sudden backward jerk, and his left hand went up involuntarily to his neck.

"Sorry, Steve," Jay apologized, "but I did tell you to sit back in your seat. At any rate we're here, safe and sound . . . except for my legs which feel as if they belong to somebody else."

Steve felt Jay's legs withdraw from beside his own. Then once more he heard the whirring sound and knew the door was being opened.

A sudden rush of night air filled the cruiser, and it felt good upon his face. He remained still, knowing that Jay would tell him when to leave. He heard Jay's soft murmurings to Flame, quickly followed by a throaty snort from the stallion.

"S-sh, Flame," Jay reprimanded the horse. "Take him out, Steve."

Steve rose to his feet, seeing nothing and wondering where he should go to find the door. He waited and finally Jay took him by the arm again.

"I keep forgetting, Steve. This way." Jay chuckled softly. "A few more steps and I won't have to lead you around like a blind man. I imagine you'll be grateful for that, too."

Steve emerged into a small clearing in a heavily wooded area. Flame jumped beside him, neighing shrilly, and Jay hushed the stallion again.

"Let's get out of here," he said to Steve, leading the way.

Steve followed, with Flame moving restlessly alongside, his head high, his eyes glaring, but never pulling upon the lines.

At the end of the clearing, Jay stopped. "Dash it," he said, "I've forgotten my bag. Hold on a minute, Steve."

Steve watched Jay run across the clearing. He sought to train his eyes to see the cruiser, if only by the slight gleam of a bubble to fix its location. But he saw nothing, and meanwhile Jay disappeared from sight long before reaching the trees.

Flame snorted again, and Steve turned back to him. The stallion's nostrils were flared widely, sniffing unfamiliar scents. Steve stroked him softly, comforting him, and Flame turned his head at the boy's touch, nuzzling his hand before once more shattering the night air with a shrill whistle.

Jay returned, carrying a large bag. "It wouldn't be wise to be found here," he told Steve anxiously. "Can't

you keep him quiet? I've done all I can, and he contin-
ues making enough noise to wake up the countryside!
We'll have the dogs on us, if he keeps it up."

Jay hurried through the trees, and Steve led Flame
after him without answering. The stallion continued his
neighing but otherwise gave Steve no trouble.

They walked a long while, emerging from the trees
to follow a deep ditch, then climbing out and entering
the woods again. Steve had no doubt that Jay knew exactly where he was going. When they finally reached a
dirt road, they were perspiring and breathing heavily.
But Flame seemed tireless; he pressed on, impatient at
their slowing footsteps, snorting loudly and neighing.

Jay said, "Let him make all the noise he wants to
now." He took a few quick breaths before adding, "I just
didn't want anyone to find us near the cruiser."

"They wouldn't be able to see it anyway," Steve
said.

"No, but they might walk into it and become
alarmed. Perhaps they'd even damage it in some way.
Then where would we be?"

Steve had no answer.

In the distance they heard dogs barking, and Flame
shrilled his challenge again.

Jay said, "He isn't pulling, is he?"

"No," Steve said. And strangely enough, the lines
were loose in his hands, even though the barking of the
dogs and the open dirt road beneath Flame's restless
hoofs should have caused the stallion to pull hard on the
lines.

"Could they find us here?" Steve asked.

"Of course. Although it isn't the villagers' custom to leave their homes at night. They're fishermen ... early risers, you know. However, what if they did come upon us walking along here? We'd only be what we look like, you know, two men and a horse."

Steve said not a word. Two men and a horse. It was as simple as that. No Blue Valley. No mother ship from a distant planet. No cruiser that had brought them here in a matter of minutes. Nothing before them but a village where people lived and faced the reality of catching fish for their livelihood, day after day. Two men and a horse, walking through the night. As simple as that.

Jay's pace slowed still more, and Steve said, "You're tired. Shall I carry your bag for a while?"

"No, thanks, Steve. You've got enough to do with Flame acting as he is. I can't understand it. He should be very quiet." Jay paused, taking a long breath before adding, "But we haven't far to go now."

Finally they were able to see the distant lights of the village, and the sea was close for they could hear the crash of waves. Once they heard shrill laughter carried on the night breeze from the village, and later music from a juke box or radio.

Flame neighed at each strange sound, but he did not rear or bolt and Steve kept him at his side.

Suddenly Jay stopped. "Well, we're here, Steve," he said.

"Where do we go?" Steve asked, seeing nothing but trees and the bare road.

"Why, right here, of course," Jay answered, turning in from the road.

Only when Steve too had stepped off the road was he aware of the graveled driveway. It circled through the trees, going in the direction of the sea. Occasionally he could see the lights of the village, and once more he heard faint music.

Flame's whistle pierced the night, and it was echoed by louder barking from the dogs.

Jay said, "I suppose that hearing all these unfamiliar noises is good for Flame. He'll get used to them and settle down, making it easier for us later."

"I guess so," Steve said. "But the people will hear him tonight for sure."

"I suppose so," Jay agreed. "But it doesn't matter. A horse is nothing unusual to them. No more than my renting this seaside home for the week-end."

Just ahead Steve saw the dim outline of a sprawling house, and closer still a small shed. "When did you rent it?" he asked.

"Yesterday. Didn't you miss me, Steve?"

"Yes, but weren't they surprised to see you?"

"Surprised?" Jay asked, turning to Steve in the darkness and smiling kindly, patiently. "The renting agents, you mean? Surprised to see a wealthy gentleman from Havana seeking a few days' rest from business problems? I'm more surprised at your asking such a question, Steve! They were pleased, very pleased, I can assure you. Their price for this house was exorbitant but I didn't quibble one bit."

Undaunted, Steve said, "But they could tell you were not one of them."

"A matter of speaking Spanish, you mean?" Jay

laughed gaily. "Again, I'm surprised at you. It's a very simple language. It just flows."

Jay turned and went to the shed. Removing a key from his pocket, he opened the doors. He turned on the light and inside Steve saw a large box stall, also a bale of hay . . . both waiting for Flame.

"Horseback riding is a sport enjoyed by many Havana businessmen," Jay said. "They love to ride along the coast. So a seaside house is not a home without a stable." He chuckled at his remark, then said, "Bring in our charge, Steve. His room and dinner await."

Flame's hoofs rang on the wood floor as he followed Steve into the shed. He reared when Jay put on the light, almost striking his head on the ceiling. When he came down he pawed the floor hard, his large eyes bright with fright.

"Put him in the stall," Jay said, alarmed and full of anxiety now. "He'll settle down there."

Steve led Flame into the roomy stall and remained beside him, trying to soothe him by words and gentle stroking. Finally he told Jay, "He'll never get used to a stall, no matter how large it is."

Jay cut the cord binding the bale of hay, and offered some to Flame. "Maybe if he eats something, Steve," he suggested.

The red stallion sniffed the hay without touching it.

Steve said, "I'll have to graze him. He won't eat this. . . . Not now, anyway."

"He will if he has nothing else," Jay said, his irritation returning. "You can take him out for grass tomorrow morning. We can do nothing more at this time, and there's no possibility of his hurting himself in such a fine big stall." He turned away. "Come on, Steve. You must be as hungry as I am."

"You go in the house," Steve said. "I'll stay here with him."

"But . . ." Jay began, bewilderment in his eyes as he looked first at Steve, then at Flame. "All right then," he said, "I'll bring something to you." Suddenly he brightened.

"Just wait until you taste what I'm cooking tonight! It's called *paella.* I picked up the recipe yesterday at lunch. It has yellow rice and bits of sausage, hot sausage, Steve . . . and chicken and clams and mussels."

Steve watched Jay hurry to the door; there the little man stopped, turning around again. "Of course you won't be sleeping here, will you? Not when you can have a comfortable bed for a change."

"I'm not leaving him," Steve answered firmly.

Jay shrugged his narrow shoulders. "Sometimes I just don't understand you at all," he said. "But have it your own way. I just thought you'd like a good night's sleep with all the work you have ahead of you." He left the shed, his voice trailing behind him.

Steve thought, *"It's a party for Jay, a big party. Eat well. Sleep well. Have fun. Soon we'll be off to the races!"* He turned to Flame, trying to quiet the stallion's mounting uneasiness. *"For us, it's different, a lot different. But I guess Jay doesn't understand. It's a detail he's forgotten."*

Later Steve heard music again, only now it was much louder, being ever so much closer. Jay had turned on the radio.

THE VISITOR

12

The *paella* had been everything Jay promised . . . savory with just the right amount of hot peppers and sausage, fresh chicken and seafood, all garnishing the steaming, yellow rice. They had eaten in the shed, straddling a bale of hay that was covered by a gaily checkered table-cloth which Jay had supplied.

"It's not exactly the way I'd planned it," Jay said. "But I dislike eating alone more than anything else. Good, isn't it?"

Steve's mouth had been too full to answer. Jay laughed, very pleased that his cooking was being so well appreciated.

Hours later, Steve lay in the straw just outside Flame's stall. His eyes were closed but he was not asleep. Sleep would come only when Flame had settled down for the night. The horse's movements within the stall never ceased, and there was no end to his neighing.

In the darkness of the shed, Steve continued talking to Flame. It made no difference what he said so long as he kept talking. Only the sound of his voice mattered, that and the rhythm.

"It's a nice, big stall, isn't it? Almost as big as my room at home, Flame. I wonder what my folks are doing tonight? Reading, I suppose, if they're not in bed by now. Unless there's a fight on, of course. Then Dad will be watching television, and Mom will be out in the kitchen to get away from it. I guess she reads more than anyone else in the world. It would be nice if she had a book of mine to read some day. I'd be proud, Flame. I sure would be."

The stallion pawed the straw and neighed loudly. There were also sounds of hay being quickly pulled from the manger and then Flame's cautious chewing.

"It's grass, all right," Steve told him, "cured grass. Not the kind you're used to, but a lot of horses eat it. Up north where it gets cold, horses eat it all winter long . . . and some who don't have any pastures to graze even eat it during the summer."

The chewing stopped and Flame began moving about the stall again.

"I'll bet Mom and Dad would be surprised if they knew I was a couple of thousand miles closer to home," Steve continued. "And they'd never believe the way I got here. Nobody I know would believe that. Yet we're here. I wish they could meet Jay. Flick, too. I wonder if the others from the ship are as nice. I'm sure they must be. They're all somewhere in our world, seeing things, and nobody even knows it. Nobody but me."

The stallion snorted. He must have had his head over the stall door, for Steve felt his warm breath.

"All right," Steve said quietly, "*you* know about them, too. Just you and me, then. I'll have to watch Jay while we're here. Not that he'd intentionally do anything wrong. But he takes an awful lot for granted sometimes. He doesn't know you as I do, Flame, in spite of everything he *does* know."

The high windows in the shed held the first gray light of dawn when Steve opened his eyes. Startled, he jumped to his feet, worried about Flame. He had slept and couldn't remember if Flame had ever settled down or not.

The shed was terribly still, and he could see nothing of Flame in the grayness of early morning. Frantically he searched for the hanging light cord. When he finally found it he pulled hard on it, his eyes on the stall. Still no movement there. No sign of Flame. Rushing to the door, he yanked it open. In the straw lay the red stallion, breathing easily. His eyes had opened as the light had struck them and now they blinked in its glare. He raised his head from the straw, neighing softly, and Steve was beside him, laughing with relief and running his hands down the long, slim neck while Flame drew his forelegs beneath him and rose.

Steve pulled the matted straw from Flame's mane, telling him how glad he was that he had rested. The stallion pulled a mouthful of hay from the rack and Steve knew then that everything was all right. He smoothed the mane and then cleaned Flame's long tail. He found himself wishing he had a brush, and he thought of the shining metal water pail Jay had left in the shed the night before. Jay must have a brush, too, somewhere around. Steve wondered how long Jay usually slept in the morning.

Picking up the pail, he refilled it, glad to see that Flame had emptied it during the night. He glanced at the hackamore hanging from a peg outside the stall. All this was far removed from the life they'd known in Blue Valley. He felt very domesticated. But at least it could be done. He had proved that much, even though he preferred what had been left behind. And he didn't have to wonder if Flame felt any differently.

A little later he slipped the hackamore over Flame's head. He noticed the rapid swaying of the long tassels even though there was no movement from Flame and no draft in the shed. For a moment he thought of the billowing, angry tapestries again and of how Jay had said, "... *everything is alive in one form or another. Nothing is ever really dead.*"

Steve took up the lines, and their warmth felt good in the early morning dampness. "If nothing is ever really dead," he thought, opening the shed doors, "then no one is ever really alone. Come on, Flame. Easy now."

The stallion stepped lightly into the heavy grayness. He sniffed the moist sea wind. Steve made no attempt to keep him quiet, for Flame's calls held neither alarm nor fright as they had during the previous evening. The stallion was sure of himself once more, and his shrill whistles carried all of his Blue Valley arrogance. His head disclosed it too, for he held it high, undaunted by the strangeness of this land.

Flame moved quickly in the dim light, and his coat, so red and glistening beneath the electric bulbs, now looked somber in color; yet his body appeared larger and more powerful. Steve let him go, holding the lines loose in his hands and allowing the stallion to choose his own grass to graze. There were few patches to Flame's liking, and he moved constantly from one place to another, his head close to the ground and nostrils sniffing.

When he stopped it was to snatch only a few blades, if any at all, then he would go on, taking Steve farther and farther away from the shed. Often, too, he would turn his head curiously about him, his eyes bright and his ears pricked up. He was wary, interested and unafraid.

Finally in a distant field Flame found the kind of grass he wanted. He grazed for many minutes while Steve watched him, wondering why this particular plot appealed to him when the grass looked no greener, no different from that which he had scorned before.

Flame grazed until he had had his fill, then he stepped forward again, his head still bent close to the ground. To Steve, who was following, Flame's actions seemed strange, since he was certain the stallion was not looking for more grass. Finally he saw what it was that Flame wanted.

The red stallion stopped before a shallow, sandy depression in the ground. Then he pulled on the lines.

Steve smiled and dropped the lines, turning Flame loose. Carefully the stallion lowered his great body and swung over on his back. He rolled from one side to another as only a slim, fit horse could do. He kicked and grunted with sheer pleasure for many minutes before getting to his feet again.

Steve, observing Flame's dusty red coat, laughed and said, "Now I *do* hope Jay brought along a brush for you. Before it wasn't so very necessary but now it is."

But Flame wasn't listening to him. He started off before Steve had finished, pulling impatiently.

"It'd be easier if I rode you," Steve said. He began looking for a place from which to mount. Flame needed the exercise. It would help matters the rest of the day if the red stallion got rid of some of his energy now.

They reached the top of a knoll and the waters of the Caribbean were before them. It was not an empty sea, for a group of fishing boats had put out from the village. They rode in a long line of brilliantly colored sails. The boats changed course just before reaching a point opposite Steve, and headed for the reef over which the waves were breaking. After they had passed through a channel and were well out to sea they spread out, moving southward.

The sun was just breaking over the horizon when Steve led Flame down the path to the beach. Flame jumped when his hoofs touched the sand for the first time but he did not pull away. He pawed the deep, granular softness of the sand, flailing it about him. Steve got out of the way, and managed to get Flame near a high rock. He stepped onto it quickly and was on Flame's back while the stallion was still occupied with the sand.

Flame whirled when he felt Steve's weight, and his legs sent the sand flying still more. It peppered his belly, and he bolted to get away from it. But the footing was too soft for swiftness of gait. Also, Steve held the lines tight; he didn't want his horse to go all out just then.

Far down the beach Steve guided Flame close to the waters where the waves had made the sand more firm. Here Flame sought more line but Steve wouldn't give it to him. The stallion snorted and shook his head. Then he bolted and for a few seconds he was free!

Steve had no intention of letting Flame continue his extended run, and finally he was able to turn the stallion's head toward the sea. Flame swerved away from the rush of waters, and Steve continued turning him. He rode him in a large circle that took them back to the sea again. After he had done this several times, Flame came to an abrupt, plunging halt.

Steve said, "That's enough."

Flame was no longer interested in running anyway. He picked up his feet high as the white, curling waves rushed to meet him. And he let them catch him, striking out playfully as the water rounded his legs. Then he became more daring, chasing each wave as it rolled back.

For many minutes Steve let Flame play with the sea, then his hands and legs moved, telling his horse what he wanted him to do. Flame was reluctant to leave the waves but he turned away, obediently going down the beach at a slow gallop.

Steve dismounted near the house. Was Jay up? he wondered. It was getting late. He didn't look forward to his trip to Havana today but there were many things he needed to know. Would he and Flame race tomorrow or would they, instead, be returning to Blue Valley?

Reaching the side door of the house, he called loudly, "Jay, are you up?"

"Come in, Steve. Come in."

The door opened and Jay was standing in the entrance, wearing pajamas and bathrobe. "Oh, my, you can't go anywhere without him, can you? Put Flame in his stall, Steve, and then come back. I'm just getting breakfast."

"I won't leave him alone," Steve said.

"My! Hasn't he settled down yet? He *looks* settled."

"We've been out."

"So early?" Jay asked. "Well, have it your way, Steve. I'll bring breakfast to you."

"I don't like to have you waiting on me."

"No trouble at all, Steve. Glad to do it, really."

"Did you bring a brush?"

"I don't use one, Steve."

"I mean for Flame."

"Oh, of course. It's in my bag. Forgetful of me not to have given it to you last night. I'll bring it along, Steve."

As Steve led Flame back to the shed, he realized that he was very reluctant to leave his horse alone with Jay while he went to Havana. Why, Jay might just go off and forget all about Flame . . . not intentionally, of course.

A little later Steve heard footsteps outside the shed. He turned as the door opened, and he said, "Jay, you mustn't forget . . ." Then he stopped abruptly, for it wasn't Jay whom he saw.

A thin, sallow face peered around the door, small eyes bright and searching. Steve's muscles tensed. He was certain the man had not expected to find any person inside the shed. But apparently the stranger knew about Flame, for he cast a quick interested glance at the stallion. Then his beady eyes fixed themselves on Steve.

"What do you want?" Steve asked.

The door opened wider and the man stepped inside, closing the door behind him. He wore a torn cotton shirt and his thick black hair grew far down on the sides of his head. Moving noiselessly on bare feet, he took several steps forward, both hands outstretched and shoulders hunched.

Steve moved toward him, very tense but unafraid. No one was going to get at Flame, and this man was no bigger than himself . . . and apparently unarmed. "What do you want?" he repeated.

Only when the stranger was less than a foot away did he speak, and then it was in Spanish, which Steve did not understand. But the man's actions made it plain that he was determined to reach Flame. His eyes were on the stallion, and he took another step closer to the stall door.

As Flame snorted, Steve attempted to stop the man. He saw the stranger's hand go quickly to his back pocket. He was certain the man was reaching either for a knife or a gun. He jumped on him, his fingers digging into the man's wrist and around it, imprisoning the hand within the pocket. His free arm swept around the thin chest, while his legs struck the stranger's stiff knees, bringing him down hard on the floor. He brought the man's other arm back, doubling it behind him and twisting it.

The stranger struggled but Steve did not release his grip; instead he tightened it even more, conscious only of a frenzy to protect his horse.

Suddenly the door opened and Jay entered, carrying

a tray of fried eggs, toast, bacon and a pot of coffee. When he saw the two struggling figures he almost dropped the tray. "What is it, Steve?" he shouted. "What's happening here?"

"Don't stand there!" Steve shouted back, for the man had managed to get one hand free.

Jay moved toward them, but he didn't put down the tray. Instead he bent over awkwardly to look at the stranger's lowered face. Then he asked in surprise, *"Qué es, Juan?"*

A torrent of angry Spanish words burst forth from the stranger while Steve sought to regain his hold of him. "Don't stand there, Jay!" he called again. "Put down that tray and help."

But Jay was laughing so he could hardly stop. Meanwhile Flame was screaming and the stranger was still shouting. Only Steve was quiet, furiously quiet.

Finally Jay managed to stop laughing. He spilled some coffee on his bathrobe and proceeded to wipe it off while he said to Steve, "Let him go. He's our *neighbor*!"

Steve kept tight hold of the man. "I don't care," he said savagely. "He tried to get to Flame!"

"What's wrong with feeding Flame a carrot?" Jay asked, starting to laugh again. He pried Steve's hand loose from the man's wrist, and withdrew a large carrot from the stranger's back pocket. Holding it directly in front of Steve's face, he said patiently, "Now let him go, Steve. He says you're hurting him very much and he's *furious.*"

Steve's arms dropped quickly to his sides, and he said, "I'm sorry. If only he'd told me."

The stranger leaned forward till their noses were almost touching, and Steve understood only the anger in the renewed outburst. Turning helplessly to Jay, he pleaded, "Tell him I didn't know, that I'm sorry."

Jay chuckled. "I guess Juan realizes by now that you don't understand Spanish." He took the man by the arm and led him to the door. Even after they were outside Steve heard and *felt* the visitor's wrath.

Later Jay returned to the shed and they ate breakfast in silence. Only when their plates were wiped clean did Jay say, "You're a very suspicious young fellow, Steve."

"I think I had a right to be," Steve answered.

"I suppose so since you don't understand Spanish," Jay agreed. "Juan lives just down the road, sort of a farmer-caretaker more than a fisherman. I met him yesterday. It was he who had the key to this place and showed me around, even did our marketing for us. I told him we'd have a horse here today. He loves them but can't afford one of his own."

Steve looked up from his plate, his eyes angry. "Don't make it any harder for me, Jay. I said I'm sorry, and I meant it."

"I apologize," Jay said kindly. "However, I just feel that you're going to get yourself into a lot of trouble by being so suspicious of these people. Or you'll make them suspicious of us by your very actions, and that's worse. Take it easy, Steve. You don't see me getting upset, and I've a lot more to conceal than you have."

Steve rose from the bale of straw and went to

Flame. "You're right," he conceded. "I'm not very good at pretending to be what I'm not."

Jay laughed. "That's understandable, Steve. You've never had occasion to do it before. Now take me, I'm an old hand at this sort of thing. And the first rule, Steve, is never to be put on the defensive. Take the offensive right away. Make it plain that you're a man of action, a man . . ."

Steve interrupted, smiling for the first time. "Didn't I do that?" he asked.

"Of course, Steve. But you didn't even know what Juan wanted here." Jay shook his head sadly. "I'm really afraid you're going to get yourself into a terrible jam in Havana today by not understanding Spanish. Perhaps . . ." He turned and faced Steve without completing his sentence.

Steve said, "You really want to go in my place, don't you? That's why you talked about my being so suspicious of the people here."

"Oh, no, Steve," Jay replied. "I'll gladly stay with Flame. Unless, of course, you'd *prefer* my going. And I'll tell you one thing, if I go no one will put anything over on me. I'll see that you race, all right." He stopped, waiting hopefully, his eyes never leaving the boy.

Steve went over to Flame, and as he stood close to him he remembered his earlier concern at leaving him alone with Jay. "Okay, Jay," he said. "I guess you *are* better equipped to go."

The little man jumped nimbly in the air, bringing the heels of his leather slippers together with a soft little click. "I'll get dressed and leave right away, Steve!" He rushed to the door, then stopped and turned around. "I do hope you won't be bored being left alone. I'll get back just as soon as I can."

Steve waited until the door closed behind Jay, then he turned to his horse. Bored? He had Flame for company, and there was a lot to think about. Tomorrow they might be going to Havana themselves.

THE WEALTHY GENTLEMAN

13

Jay was in no hurry to reach Havana once he had left Steve and Flame behind. He was enjoying his close contact with people from Earth and their acceptance of him as one of their own. He was happy, too, over the way he had handled Steve. Of course, everything he had said was quite true. With his background he could handle the racetrack officials far better than an inexperienced boy. However, there was no need to think of that little job just yet. All that mattered now was that he was on his own and could enjoy himself as much as he liked.

He had been standing in the aisle of the crowded Havana-bound bus for a long while, and his fine black homburg hat had been knocked off his head several times. But he had taken the jostling from the other passengers very well. In fact, he had joked about it to those standing close by. At first they hadn't laughed with him, feeling perhaps that he was not one of them. Oh, not

144

that they knew he was from Alula. Indeed not, nothing like that. Rather it was his clothes—his fine dark hat, suit and tie and his white shirt with the stiff collar—these and the silver-handled cane he carried must have given them the impression that he was a very wealthy man, and they had been afraid to joke with him.

All this had changed, however, when a sudden stop had thrown him down hard to the floor, and a very fat woman had landed on top of him. Of course she had hurt him dreadfully, and he must have looked ridiculous while two grinning men had pulled the lady to her feet. Everyone had laughed at his frightful predicament. After that it had been easy to get along with them.

Halfway to Havana he found that most passengers were changing buses, and he decided to go along with these very nice people.

"But you were going to the city," the man next to him said in very bad Spanish. "This is not the way. We go to work in the factories."

"I'll go along," Jay said quietly, slurring his Spanish, just as the man had done. "I'm in no hurry, and I enjoy your company very much."

The man shook his head sadly but smiled at the same time. The other passengers too, Jay noted, were pleased that he was accompanying them, for they called out and made very pleasant remarks to him.

The other bus was waiting for them and he was very flattered when his new friends insisted upon his having a seat this time.

He never remembered a more wonderful trip than the one that followed. Oh, it was true they all made much fun of him and his apparent wealth. They told him that he would never get a job in the factory wearing such beautiful clothes. They passed his black homburg around, each one trying it on while he in turn wore their straw hats. They even took his cane and he thought for a while that he would never see it again. But eventually it came back to him, just as his hat did.

It was all a great deal of fun, and he was sorry when it came to an end. By separate large groups the passengers left the bus at factories along the way, and finally he was alone and the driver asked if he were going to spend the day with him. Only then did Jay think of Havana and the business at hand.

Glancing at his gold watch he said impatiently, "I must get to Havana immediately."

The driver smiled tolerantly. "Then you must ride back with me to where you got on. Once there you must wait for still another bus."

"How long will all that take?" Jay asked anxiously, getting to his feet.

"It will not be soon," the driver said. "I do not leave here for another thirty minutes."

"Is there no other way to reach Havana?" Jay looked out the windows. "Are there no taxis?" On the gate of a nearby factory he saw a huge poster announcing the great International Race to be run the next day at El Dorado Park, and his impatience to reach the city broke out afresh. "There must be cars to hire out here," he said.

The bus driver smiled, and his eyes surveyed Jay's fine clothes again. "If there are any around they will find you," he said.

"But what do you suggest I do?" Jay asked.

"Get out and walk," the driver said. "Something should happen very quickly."

"Thank you. Thank you very much," Jay answered in his finest Spanish.

He walked past the factory and down the asphalt-topped road, looking for a taxi. But the only signs of activity came from the belching smokestacks. He felt very much alone with everyone working but himself. He hurried along, climbing a steep hill. At the top he could see nothing before him but great fields of sugar cane on either side of the road. He knew then that it would do no good to walk aimlessly along, waiting for something to happen, as the bus driver had suggested.

As he stood there, his eyes on the long empty stretch of road, his ears listening for the sound of a car, he became more nervous than ever. It was most frustrating! He looked up at the sky. There was a large black buzzard circling just above him. Oh, he could get to Havana all right. But his flying was very much against the rules on such a trip as this. They'd leave him here if they ever found out. He'd never see home again.

Pearly beads of perspiration appeared on his forehead and he swept them angrily away. His Earth body functioned in a very strange manner indeed. . . .

He waited longer, but not patiently. Well, if there was no alternative he had to take a chance of getting to Havana the only way left, although he certainly wished . . . He looked at the buzzard again. It was such a big bird. . . . Suddenly he heard the noise of a car's engine, and with great relief turned toward it.

The car came up the hill, hissing and rattling under

the strain of making the steep ascent. Jay stepped out in the middle of the road and raised his hand high in the air.

The car stopped, but the driver, barely glancing at Jay, got out and went forward to remove the cap from the steaming radiator.

Jay jumped back at sight of the geyser of steam that emerged, and the man laughed at him. He was still laughing when he went to the back of the car and returned with a large can of water which he poured into the hot radiator. Then he put back the cap and turned to Jay, studying him closely for the first time.

His eyes brightened as he scrutinized Jay's fine clothes and the silver-handled cane. "Sir," he said anxiously, "you are in trouble, and in need of help?"

"I must reach Havana at once," Jay said, using his finest, richest Spanish. He had met this type of man before, and had not forgotten how best to impress him. "If I may hire your car and services . . ."

"But of course," the man interrupted, opening the car door with a great flourish. "We will waste no time in further words while not in transit. I understand your emergency and quickly respond to your bidding." He hurried Jay into the car, happy that no fare for the trip had been set and he could demand his own figure upon their arrival in Havana.

Jay made no attempt to carry on a conversation with this man as he had done with his good friends on the bus. He was a sullen person who would not have helped him, or anyone else for that matter, without expecting and obtaining a very high price for his services.

While the man talked on and on, Jay looked out at

the countryside, trying hard to concentrate on the fields of cane, the citrus fruit orchards and finally the long avenues that were shaded by laurel trees, ceibas and stately royal palms. Eventually, the road descended to the sea and a light wind brought the smell of dead sea grass lying in the hot sun. He glanced at his watch again, and seeing that it was almost noon he fidgeted more than before.

"It won't be long now," the man said, letting the car roll recklessly down the hill. "See, there is the dome of the Capitol!"

Jay only nodded, not sharing the man's jubilation at sight of the city. The important thing was that other cars were now on the road, most of them passing quickly by. If anything happened to the sputtering engine he would not be without further conveyance.

From having studied the ship's screen the day before, he knew where they were in Havana. The towering National Hotel was near the white dome of the Capitol, and then he could see the Morro Castle, and many other buildings, all looking clean and beautiful in the bright noonday sun.

For a moment he thought of the fun it would be just to sit quietly in some restaurant, watching the people that passed . . . or, better still, walking leisurely through the streets, talking to passers-by. He turned his gaze away from the buildings to watch a ship leaving the harbor. Still farther beyond were some fishing smacks. His eyes remained on the dark line made by the Gulf Stream, and he thought of the lonely island from which Steve and Flame had come. . . . Then he remembered all he had promised the boy.

"I'll be getting out soon," he told the driver.

"But, sir, this is only the suburbs."

"I know," Jay answered, "but there is no need of my going downtown. I must go directly to El Dorado Park."

"The racetrack? Then I will take you there. It is a much longer ride, of course."

"No, I will get a taxi, thank you. There's one now."

"But there is no need," the man said insolently. "I can take you there as well. And the fare . . ."

"No," Jay insisted, "a taxi suits me better."

"Better?" the man asked irritably.

Jay's face flushed. "I mean that it will get me there faster. Please stop now, and I will pay you."

The driver jammed the foot brake. "I will have to charge you for the whole trip," he said, smiling. "All the way to El Dorado Park, since it is there that you intended to go."

"That's perfectly all right," Jay said, glad that the car had stopped and he was able to get out. Opening the door, he hailed a taxi, and then turned to the man in the car. "You've been most kind," he said, taking a bill from his wallet and handing it to him.

The driver looked at the bill, and said nothing. It was more than he would have asked for, and he had intended to charge a great deal. When he took his eyes off the bill, he saw his wealthy passenger climbing into the taxi. "Sir," he called, "one moment, please."

Jay waited, wondering what the man wanted. Surely he had paid him well.

The man's eyes were bright, almost frantic, Jay thought.

"Yes?" Jay said.

"Sir, perhaps you know the winner of the great race tomorrow? No doubt you are a famous horseman. And it would help me greatly to know the name of the winning horse."

Jay closed the taxi door. "It would help me too," he said through the open window.

"But, sir . . ."

The taxi moved, and Jay told the driver, "El Dorado Park, please. And skirt the traffic. I'm in a great hurry."

Jay sat back, content that he had done right in transferring to the taxi. Not only because he would reach the Park much faster, but also because he would make a much better impression arriving there in a taxi rather than in the unfashionable vehicle he had just left. The latter was important because he well knew how much emphasis was placed upon such things by Earthmen. And, of course, he must do his best to impress the racetrack officials with his importance from the very beginning. Yes, he must take the offensive immediately, just as he had told Steve.

He relaxed, unaware of the mounting speed of the taxi, the blaring horn and the many near accidents that were avoided as he was taken from one residential section to another. Instead he was thinking that what he should do at once was to telephone the track and advise the officials of his coming. This, too, would be most impressive, especially if he allowed them to think that it was his secretary who was calling.

" 'I am calling for Mr. . . . Mr. . . .' I must have a name," he thought. "One worthy of such an occasion. I believe I'll be Dutch . . . yes, that'll be just fine. I'll say I'm from the Dutch West Indies. What's the name of that Dutch island off the coast of Venezuela? Curaçao, that's it. Now for my name. I'll call myself Van Oss . . . yes, I like that. I like it very much. 'Hello. Hello. I am calling for Mr. Henry Van Oss of Curaçao.' Umm. Hm. Very good."

Jay saw the drug store on the corner just ahead. Surely he'd find a public telephone there. "Driver," he called, "stop here a moment. I want to make a call."

A little later Jay returned to the taxi, very pleased with his telephone conversation with Mr. Garcia-Pena, Race Secretary of El Dorado Park. Mr. Garcia-Pena had been most gracious. He was awaiting Mr. Van Oss of Curaçao with the utmost pleasure, eager to assist him in every way possible, whatever his wishes might be.

Jay smiled as the taxi moved on again. *Whatever his wishes might be.* Little did Mr. Garcia-Pena realize what Mr. Van Oss would ask of him!

"Sir . . ." the driver began, turning his head around so he could look at Jay.

They almost collided with a passing car, and Jay said quickly, "Please keep your eyes on the road!"

Chastened, the driver obeyed. Then, without taking his eyes off the boulevard, he said, "May I ask if you're an owner of a horse in tomorrow's great race?"

"In a sense," Jay answered, enjoying the man's deference. "Yes, I suppose you might call me a part-owner. Although we're undecided about starting tomorrow. I've only just arrived."

"The fifty-thousand-dollar purse would decide me pretty quick about starting," the driver said, laughing.

"Yes," Jay admitted, "it *is* an impressive purse."

"I guess everybody's figuring on Kingfisher taking it home with him."

"Kingfisher?" Jay asked.

"Sure . . . the *big* horse from the United States. He's handicap champion there, as I guess you know."

"No, I didn't know," Jay answered. "I haven't kept in touch with races in the United States. You said his name is Kingfisher?"

"Yes," the driver said. "It's a good name, don't you think?"

"Kingfisher," Jay repeated. "Yes, the name appeals to me, too."

"Then you like him for the big race, sir?"

"I like anything that has to do with birds," Jay answered quietly.

The man glanced back at him. "What have birds got to do with it?"

"Watch the road, please," Jay repeated nervously. "Nothing, I suppose . . . except that kingfisher is also the name of a bird."

"It's an easy name to remember."

"Yes," Jay said thoughtfully. "But come to think of it, it's strange that they should give such a name to a horse. A kingfisher has very weak feet, and I'm sure you're acquainted with the old saying, 'No feet, no horse.' "

"You don't have to worry about his feet, sir. They've carried him a long way. He's six years old now and hasn't been beaten since he was three."

"I'm surprised," Jay said. "A kingfisher's feet just don't stand up under hard going for a very long time."

Bewildered, the driver looked back at his passenger again. "*This* Kingfisher's a horse," he said.

Jay said nothing more for the main entrance to El Dorado Park and the high fence surrounding it were directly ahead. He settled back in his seat, concerned now only with Mr. Garcia-Pena and all that he had to say to him.

They passed through the gate, and Jay wouldn't let himself look at the gigantic grandstand and clubhouse or, a little later, at the horses being walked beside the stable sheds. He shut his ears, too, to the loud voices of caretakers calling to each other and the neighs and nickering of the horses.

Oh, he wanted so very much to look, to listen, for he had waited a terribly long time to enjoy once more the activity of a racetrack. But today was not the day. Tomorrow, yes, but not today. He must think only of his coming session with Mr. Garcia-Pena. He must be fully prepared to outwit the Race Secretary no matter how formidable an opponent Mr. Garcia-Pena might turn out to be. He must not return to Steve with anything but the happiest news, that Flame would be going to the post tomorrow. Nothing less would do, so every move, every remark, must be well planned. He must not let Mr. Garcia-Pena put him on the defensive at any time.

"Sir, are you not getting out?"

Jay glanced at the driver, then with further surprise he saw that the taxi was parked in front of a low building. He wondered how many minutes they'd been parked there.

"Why, yes . . . yes, of course," he answered, a little flustered. He got out of the taxi, furious with himself for his hesitancy and embarrassment. This wouldn't do at all. This was not a good start for what he had to do.

Lifting his cane deftly with a quick, confident snap of the wrist, he told the driver to wait, and then walked into the building.

THE INVITATION

14

Jay did not have long to wait for the Race Secretary to see him. And as he waited he was thoroughly at ease and, indeed, nonchalant, sitting comfortably in a deep leather chair with his legs crossed and his fine black homburg balanced on one knee. His long fingers drummed the silver head of his cane but not impatiently . . . or so it would have seemed to an onlooker.

In a little while a girl emerged from the inner office, smiled and said that Mr. Garcia-Pena would see him. Jay did not leave his chair, but smiled graciously in return and waited for Mr. Garcia-Pena to appear and escort him inside. There was an uneasy moment or two, then the girl disappeared within the office and seconds later a small dark-haired man stood in the doorway.

"Mr. Van Oss?" the Race Secretary asked, smiling.

Jay rose to his feet, nodding graciously but not smiling. "Mr. Garcia-Pena?" He waited until the man crossed the floor to greet him, and then they went into the office.

For a few minutes more Jay allowed Mr. Garcia-Pena to scrutinize him while they discussed the unusually hot day, the lack of a breeze and the little rain there had been.

"Of course," and Mr. Garcia-Pena smiled, "we would not like to have it rain tomorrow. We're expecting a tremendous crowd for the International."

"Naturally," Jay returned, still aloof and unsmiling. He recrossed his knees, fingering the knife-edged crease of his trousers.

"If you don't mind my saying so," the Race Secretary continued, "you speak beautiful Spanish, Mr. Van Oss. It is most unusual to hear, for most of our visitors' Spanish is not . . . well, shall I say not very well spoken?"

"Thank you," Jay said, turning abruptly from the man to look at the portraits of horses on the walls.

There was a long moment of strained silence, then the Race Secretary moved some papers on his desk and said, "You didn't mention the purpose of your visit over the phone, Mr. Van Oss."

"No, I thought it best to wait," Jay said, "since it could only be done here, and will take but a few minutes of your time. I have a horse that I wish to enter in the International."

In the pause that followed, the smile that had been forming at the corners of the Race Secretary's mouth died. He looked straight into his visitor's eyes, and found himself thinking of his children . . . or, rather, of the glass marbles with which they played. This man's eyes had the same cloudy, agate-like quality and still they were clear. Colorless, yet with thin bands of color running through them; again, like the glass marbles. Uneasy, Mr. Garcia-Pena turned back to his papers.

As if from a distance he heard his visitor say, "The horse's name is Flame. I suppose you'll want that for the program."

Mr. Garcia-Pena looked up to find the man's cane raised and then drumming the carpet lightly. He chose to stare at the cane rather than to meet those eyes again. Somehow, just looking into them made it very difficult for him to concentrate.

"If there is an entry fee, I'll pay it now," Jay said. "So if you will tell me the amount . . ."

Mr. Garcia-Pena continued staring at the cane. "Five hundred dollars is the fee to start, but . . ." He had never seen such beautiful, highly polished silver as that on the cane's head. It seemed almost to glow with life . . . and so soft that it looked molten. His eyes were playing tricks on him, he decided. No metal was so pliable that it could be manipulated with the fingers, as seemed to be the case here.

Mr. Garcia-Pena smiled at his thoughts. He was being very silly. "I'm afraid, Mr. Van Oss, that what you ask is out of the question," he said graciously.

His visitor acted as if he had not heard, for he began taking money out of his wallet.

"This will cover the entry fee," Jay said, placing the bills on the desk. "Now if you'll just tell me the time we go to the post . . ."

Mr. Garcia-Pena was no longer smiling. "Please sit down again, Mr. Van Oss. You see . . ."

"I'm sorry but I have an appointment," Jay said urgently. "You have the entrance money, paid in full.

There is nothing else required by the conditions of the race as advertised." He pushed the bills toward the center of the desk, hoping Mr. Garcia-Pena would at least look at them.

But the Race Secretary, ignoring the money, had turned and pressed a button on the office intercom. "Dora," he said to his secretary, "have Mario come in immediately." Then, to his visitor, "Please sit down," he repeated. "You see, Mr. Van Oss, what you're asking is ridiculous."

"Ridiculous?" Jay's tone of voice matched the sudden sternness of his face. "Are you or are you not running the International Race tomorrow?"

"Of course, of course. But you see . . ."

Jay drew his head up scornfully. "I see nothing, Mr. Garcia-Pena, except my entry fee on your desk."

The man's eyes implored him to sit down, to listen, but Jay turned toward the door. "If you won't tell me what time they go to the post, I'll get the information from your secretary," he said curtly.

"But this race is by invitation only," the man said.

Jay didn't answer, and kept moving toward the door. He was reaching for the knob when the door opened and a tall young man entered.

"Ah, Mario," Mr. Garcia-Pena said, "just in time. I want you to meet Mr. Van Oss, from Curaçao. He's a little confused over the conditions of the race tomorrow and I thought you could help me straighten him out." Then, to Jay, "This is Mr. Santos, Mr. Van Oss. He's our Publicity Director."

Mr. Santos held out his hand, and Jay shook it without returning the man's brisk smile. He felt confident that he could handle Mr. Santos. Except for his high-sounding title, there was nothing about him that commanded respect.

Jay could see at a glance that Mr. Santos was ambitious. Eager and enterprising, he would not be aloof to a suggestion or two that might take him a step closer to whatever goal he had in mind. As Jay took in the mustache that Mr. Santos was beginning to grow, he wondered if this young man's ambition was to sit behind Mr. Garcia-Pena's luxurious desk.

"Please sit down," the Race Secretary urged Jay again.

Jay smiled understandingly and shrugged his shoulders. "If you will not waste time then, Mr. Garcia-Pena."

"This will take only a few minutes," the Race Secretary said placatingly. "Mario, will you please take the chair next to Mr. Van Oss? I may need your help to explain matters fully."

"There should be little to explain," Jay said abruptly. "The race is tomorrow, and the entry fee has been paid. You have it there on your desk. I don't see . . ."

Mr. Garcia-Pena picked up the bills. "But again I'd like to say that our race is by invitation only. After all, Mr. Van Oss, we just couldn't allow any horse to . . ." He paused and smiled sheepishly.

There was no answering smile from Jay. "Your posters made no mention of that condition," he said sternly. "No mention that you'd invited *only* the horses you wanted to race in the International. You advised the public that the International Race was *Open to the World.*"

The Race Secretary turned to Mr. Santos, seeking assistance, but the Publicity Director avoided his gaze and continued looking at their visitor. "Well, in a sense it is open to the world," the Secretary said awkwardly, "but by invitation only."

Jay uncrossed his knees, stomping his cane hard on the floor. "You can't have it both ways," he said. "My attorneys will . . ." He rose quickly to his feet and, just as he had hoped and had rather expected, the Publicity Director rose, too.

"Mr. Van Oss, please . . . ," Mr. Santos said. "I'm certain we can handle this without any, ah, legal difficulties."

Jay studied the man's large frame that was so sparingly covered with flesh. It made him think of a heron, especially since Mr. Santos had the kind of head that perfected the illusion. It was very large, and his nose was long and beaked. Jay was staring at the man's high forehead with the brown, well-groomed hair growing above it when Mr. Santos graciously placed a hand on his arm.

"Please sit down, Mr. Van Oss," the Publicity Director said, his voice as polished as his hair. "We, of course, had no idea that anyone would object to the conditions of our race. We simply sent invitations to the owners of the world's fastest horses, hoping they'd accept. Fortunately eight of them did, and we have a field tomorrow that will make racing history for Cuba."

"And for El Dorado Park," Mr. Garcia-Pena

interrupted. "The race will be featured in every newspaper in the world."

"Naturally," the Publicity Director said. "It's what I counted on after all my work."

Jay allowed himself to be seated in the big chair again. "Then you have no objection to my horse racing?" he asked insistently, meeting the Race Secretary's gaze.

Once more Mr. Garcia-Pena turned helplessly to his Publicity Director.

This time the Publicity Director was ready with a suggestion. "Could we not issue another invitation . . . one to Mr. Van Oss, Eduardo?"

The Race Secretary rose to his feet, then quickly sat down again. "The United States Jockey Club wouldn't like it, Mario! You know that as well as I do. After all, we have two horses here from the States, and if we issue a last-minute invitation such as you're suggesting, why . . ."

"The United States Jockey Club is not running *this* race," the Publicity Director returned quietly. "I see no reason why we can't invite any horse we please, providing . . ."

There was a moment of heavy silence and then Jay turned to him. "Providing what, Mr. Santos?"

His face cupped in his hands, chin outthrust, Mr. Santos was staring into space thoughtfully. "Providing, Mr. Van Oss, that you have a horse that will not embarrass us."

"Embarrass?" Jay repeated.

The Publicity Director's eyes were beginning to shine with excitement. "We must be sure, Mr. Van Oss, that your horse will give a creditable performance . . . if not in the race at least during the post parade. He must compliment our field, for the world will be watching."

Once more the Race Secretary rose to his feet, his face angry now. "You mean, Mario, you'd go along with this? What Mr. Van Oss has asked is impossible! We'll be the laughingstock of the world. How do we know what he'd send onto the track? A burro, maybe, that would bray in our faces!"

"That, Eduardo, we must find out, of course," the Publicity Director returned quietly. "But I've been thinking of all the publicity that we might obtain from this late entry of Mr. Van Oss's. After all, we did announce that our race is open to the world, as Mr. Van Oss has reminded us. What objection could anyone have to our acceptance of his horse, even at this late date, since he is willing to pay five hundred dollars to start?

"Better still, don't you know what such startling news will do for us? Can't you see it in every paper tomorrow? It will make headlines, Eduardo! It will have an air of mystery that we'll do our best to maintain. Through the press services we'll announce to the world that an unexpected entry from . . ."

The Publicity Director turned eagerly to Jay. "From where, Mr. Van Oss? Where is your horse from?"

Jay smiled, enthusiastically going along with the Director's plan. "Wouldn't the Windward Islands be enough?" he asked. "It would add to the mystery."

"Yes, of course," Mr. Santos agreed excitedly. "From the Windward Islands, from the area of the Caribbean Sea!" Then, to the Race Secretary, "We can say that he is *our* representative in the International, since we have no other. I assure you we'll get publicity such as we've never had before! An unknown *Island* horse meeting the champions of the world! Think of it, Eduardo!"

The Race Secretary went to the window. "You're being ridiculous, Mario. You're making a farce out of a race among the world's fastest horses. Isn't it enough that we have managed to get them together *without all this*?"

The Publicity Director went hurriedly after him and placed an arm about his friend's shoulders. "Eduardo, you don't understand," he said quietly. "The race itself will be the finest ever run. And you have arranged it . . . you and you alone. But please remember that even the greatest races are made more memorable by unusual stories that are written in advance. Have you forgotten how much publicity we received as a result of my suggestion that the purse money be hung from the finish wire?"

Jay saw the Race Secretary nod his head in answer, and his own interest quickened. "Did I understand you to say you're hanging the money from the finish wire?" he asked.

The Publicity Director turned to him. "You must have read about that, Mr. Van Oss. It was in *every* newspaper. . . ."

"No," Jay said, "I haven't seen a paper in some time. Tell me about it."

"Briefly, the money will be sewn in a purse, which will be given to the winner immediately following the race. It's the way they did it long ago, and that's how the term 'purse' originated in racing terminology. You've no idea the amount of publicity we've received since the story went out."

"I guess I haven't," Jay said quietly. And how convenient, he thought, for him and Steve. All they had to do was to collect the purse after the race and leave. Lovely, just lovely . . . and so convenient.

The Publicity Director continued, "Go along with me, Eduardo, on this one last request before tomorrow's race. An unknown horse from the Islands is just what we need to stimulate further world interest in our race. I can have the news release sent out this afternoon. Every wire service, every radio and television station will carry it!" He waved his arms in the air, and Jay was reminded of the long, flopping wings of a heron in flight.

Resignedly the Race Secretary returned to his desk. "I must see this horse first," he said in a very tired voice. "Where is he, Mr. Van Oss?"

Jay jumped to his feet. "Not far from here," he said. "I have a taxi waiting. Come along."

The Waiting

15

Steve slid off the bale of straw on which he had been sitting, and went to the door again. Still no sign of Jay, and the sun was close to setting. For a moment he watched the wind chase the heavy ragged clouds across the sky. It could rain either tonight or tomorrow.

He closed the door, shutting out the dying brilliance of the sun, and returned to Flame. The stallion had his head over the stall door, eyes alert as he watched every move Steve made.

Steve said, "Wet footing wouldn't make any difference to you. I wonder about the others?"

All day long he had thought of nothing but the race, preparing Flame and himself for it. Soon after Jay's departure he had cast aside any doubts and uncertainties as to their racing in the International. A man who had taken them this far would not be stopped by the conditions of a race. It was only a matter of waiting, and soon—tomorrow—the waiting would end.

"It'll be up to us alone then, Flame . . . just you and

me. No Jay to help us once we're on the track. But we'll go just as we do in Blue Valley. Oh, it'll be different, a lot different, for both of us. There'll be noise and people . . . and other stallions too, Flame. But you'll do what I ask, won't you?"

Flame let go a couple of kicks against the wooden sides of his stall, and then reached over the half-door, taking hold of Steve's shirt in play.

Steve patted him, at the same time thoughtfully eyeing the bitless bridle which hung from a peg beside the door. It would be of some help in guiding Flame once the stallion stepped onto the track. But he must not put too much confidence in the bridle. Only his voice and hands, his love for Flame and the stallion's love for him would keep the great horse under control. Even then . . . yes, even then nothing was certain. He had no assurance that Flame would listen to him as he always had done before. The sight of other stallions, Flame's natural instinct to fight, might well bring on insurmountable problems. But it was a risk he had to take, and he accepted the challenge willingly.

He rubbed the stallion's muzzle and Flame released his shirt without drawing back. "I want the world to see how fast you are, Flame," he said softly. "I don't think you'll mind at all once we get going. You'll be as anxious to beat them as I am. Once we're on our way you'll know what it's all about. You'll race because it's the most natural thing in the world for you to do."

He believed everything he told Flame. He was impatient for Jay to return, for the night to pass, for the moment when he would ride Flame onto the track. It was the *waiting* that he hated.

As he looked at the hackamore again, he wished for a moment that it were an ordinary bridle that hung there. If it had been he could have undone all the fasteners, separating every movable part; then he could have spent a lot of time carefully cleaning each piece of leather with sponge and soap. It would have kept him busy. It would have helped a lot.

He took down the bitless bridle, his hands fingering the long tassels that were as fine as spun gold. He examined the breathing, living fibers as he turned the hackamore over, searching for any marks of sweat that might have stained it during the morning ride or any grains of sand that might cause Flame discomfort when he wore it again. But the bitless bridle was as unsoiled as on the day Jay had given it to him. His hands tightened about it, and a warmer, deeper red flooded the fibers. He was comforted by the warmth, but still he wished it were an ordinary bridle so he might have spent some time in cleaning it.

Finally he put it back on the peg, and turned again to Flame. For a moment he thought of unbraiding the stallion's long forelock and doing it over again. But he had already done that three times. Lightly he pushed Flame's head a little to the side so he could look into the stall. The bedding was clean, so there was nothing to be done there, either.

Across the stallion's back, just draping his barrel, was the folded red cooler Jay had brought along. Steve thought of pulling it up around Flame's neck, then rejected the idea. The stallion hadn't minded the blanket earlier and there was little likelihood of his objecting to it now.

For want of anything better to do, Steve went into the stall and, drawing the cooler high up, pinned it snugly around Flame's neck. Flame nipped at the edges, then lost interest. A new idea had come to him. He wanted to leave the stall.

"Not now," Steve said. "Not until tomorrow."

Flame stepped around him, and the draped blanket billowed and changed color with his movements. Steve thought of *the room* again, and the great tapestries hanging on the walls. Uneasy, he removed the cooler from Flame's back. The weather was too warm for it anyway, and there were no drafts in the shed.

He was turning away from the stall when the door of the shed opened and Jay stepped inside. Steve was about to run toward him when he noticed the two strangers standing in the doorway behind Jay.

With a gesture, Jay signaled to Steve to move away from the stall, and then he said graciously to the men, "Come in, gentlemen. Here he is."

Steve did as he had been bid, seeking enlightenment in Jay's eyes. But Jay avoided his gaze, and now spoke only in Spanish so Steve couldn't understand a word that was said. He saw the men approach the stall with Jay to look at Flame. They didn't go too close for Flame had his ears swept back. Yet they were anxious to see his body and legs, for they stepped to one side, peering into the stall.

Jay turned on the light so they could get a good look at Flame. The two men were pleased with what they saw, Steve could tell, for they nodded in agreement to almost everything Jay said. It was Jay who did all the talking, and not once did the visitors pay any attention to Steve. The gaunt, gangling man was especially impressed with Flame, for being taller he had a better view of the inside of the stall. His eyes were bright and he kept rubbing his long, bony hands together vigorously.

Steve wondered who they were and why Jay had brought them, but he knew better than to ask just then. He moved farther away from them, knowing it was what Jay wanted of him.

Finally the visit neared its close, and there was a brief discussion among the three as they turned from the stall and walked slowly to the door.

Steve waited until they were outside, then went to the door himself. From where he stood he saw the taxi, and the two men shaking hands with Jay. The smaller of the visitors wore a sober expression, but he seemed to be in full agreement with his friend. Steve wished he understood Spanish. Well, soon Jay would explain what it all meant.

The men stepped into the taxi, and the door closed behind them. Jay gave the driver a bill, and called, *"Hasta la vista,"* to the departing visitors.

As the driver looked at the bill Jay had given him, he exclaimed, *"Mil gracias, Señor! . . . Mil gracias!"*

Jay waved them off, then turned to Steve. For a moment he just looked at the boy, his face seeming to glow from the unusual brightness of his eyes. There was no need for Steve to ask if the trip to Havana had been successful.

"We're in, Steve!" Jay finally said.

"I know," the boy answered. "All I have to do is look at you to know."

"Of course, of course," Jay agreed jubilantly.

Together they walked into the shed, and Jay flung his black hat onto the bale of straw. "They had to see Flame before they'd agree to his starting in the International. Think of it, Steve," he went on, "they were afraid he might not look well in the post parade! That was their only worry, for they don't consider an untried horse as a serious contender in such a race. Oh, what a surprise they'll get, Steve . . . especially that Mr. Santos! He was the one who looked so much like a heron, you'll recall. And in his mind the only reason our horse has been accepted is that it will give him a chance to write some good publicity stories tonight. But it's just as well for us that Mr. Santos is thinking along those lines; otherwise we might not be racing tomorrow."

"What is he going to do?" Steve asked.

"Mr. Santos is going to tell the world that an unknown, unproven horse will face the champions in tomorrow's great International."

"Oh, Jay . . ." Steve began, the color leaving his face.

"Don't worry," Jay said quickly. "I told him nothing about Flame or you. Furthermore, Steve, he didn't want to know anything. That's part of it. The mystery, I mean. That's the angle Mr. Santos is depending upon to gain publicity in the newspapers, radio and on television. An unknown horse from the Windward Islands will race against the world's fastest horses! A late entry! An Island Stallion! Oh, that Mr. Santos knows his job, all right. Why, he's even arranged to hang the purse money from the finish wire. This race has been tailor-made for us, Steve . . . and so has Mr. Santos!"

Too many facts in too short a time. Steve walked to

the back of the shed. He didn't want to hear any more. That he and Flame were to race the next day was enough.

Jay's voice became louder, but Steve tried not to listen.

"I'm sorry that it was necessary to be discourteous and ignore you when I arrived, Steve. But you see, I didn't want them to take a good look at you. No one must be able to recognize you later as the person who rode Flame in the big race. Tomorrow morning I'll fix you up so your own mother wouldn't know you."

Details, important details, all of which Jay enjoyed doing so much. But to Steve, just then, nothing mattered except the actual running of the race.

"I must go to the village now," Jay continued excitedly, "and rent a truck for tomorrow. I hope you won't mind being left alone again, Steve."

"No, I don't mind . . . not at all."

Jay had not been gone very long when the sky darkened and a peal of thunder came rolling in from the sea. Steve listened to it, wondering if the storm would break before Jay reached the village. Jay would hate to get his fine clothes wet. And would he have enough foresight to get a closed truck in case it continued to rain the next day?

The shed was illuminated by a sudden flash of lightning, and then swift angry pellets of rain began falling on the tin roof. Steve's eyes became accustomed to the darkness and he made out Flame's head over the stall door. He went to him as the lightning came again and the storm in all its fury burst upon them.

The rain didn't stop until shortly after Steve awakened the next morning. He watered Flame, then went to the shed door, opening it to look at the gray, sweeping clouds. There was little chance of the sun's breaking through such an overcast. Parked near the shed was the small closed van which Jay had driven home the night before during the storm. They had bedded it down well with straw. It was ready for Flame.

He returned to his horse, offering him a bale of hay through which the stallion sniffed, searching for the particular grasses that pleased him most. As he pulled them forth, chewing slowly, his eyes remained on Steve.

The boy said, "I know you'd rather go outside and graze, so let's do it."

A few minutes later he led Flame from the shed. He took him over to the truck, and with flared nostrils and bright eyes Flame walked around it, sniffing the sides.

Then Steve mounted his horse, his hands light on the reins as he took him down the driveway.

"Easy, Flame. No running this morning."

Turning into the road, he let Flame go into a slow, easy gallop and his bare hoofs made soft, sucking sounds in the mud. The stallion asked for more rein but didn't demand it. The wind had freshened and Flame held his head high, enjoying his early morning exercise. His strides gradually lengthened and he chose the side of the road that was fetlock-deep in mud. Not once did he falter or slip.

Steve needed no reassurance of Flame's ability to handle himself in such footing. He had only to think of Blue Valley and the many times he had ridden his horse through the slimy, dangerous marsh to know there were few animals in the world more sure-footed than Flame.

He wondered about the other horses in the race. Would they take to this kind of going?

"Easy, Flame," he said again.

The stallion listened to Steve and there was no further lengthening of his strides. Steve stroked him, and turned him off the road, guiding him to the place where Flame had found the grass most to his liking the day before. Dismounting, Steve walked alongside his horse. He was glad to be away from the shed, for it helped in the matter of waiting. He wondered how long Jay would sleep this morning, and what time they would leave for Havana. Probably not until shortly after noon, for Jay had said last night that they shouldn't get there much before the race.

Post time was at three o'clock. Soon the waiting would come to an end.

Steve took his time returning to the shed, walking Flame all the way back. There was no sign of Jay when he arrived. The house was quiet and the shades were drawn. If Jay was waiting for the sun to awaken him this morning he would sleep a long time. The sky hadn't changed from its earlier leaden gray, although the force of the wind had abated.

As Steve lowered the tailgate of the van, he let it fall with a loud bang, hoping the noise would wake Jay.

"Come, boy," he said, leading Flame to the tailgate. It was a steeper ascent than Steve would have liked for his horse but an easy climb compared to some of the trails over which he had ridden Flame. He was confident the stallion would follow him.

Flame hesitated at the foot of the tailgate, his eyes searching the dark interior of the van. It was this that bothered him, Steve knew. He made his way up into the van and then stood inside, slowly moving the lines. "Come, Flame," he repeated.

The stallion's forelegs moved onto the wood, and then he stopped again, looking past Steve. Again the boy called him, and after a short pause there was a quick lurching of his body as he gathered himself for the ascent. He raised his head a little too high when he reached the top, and bumped into the roof. For a second he was alarmed by the sudden blow and the close confines of the truck. He sought to rear but Steve held his head down, talking to him all the while.

Finally Steve led him farther into the truck, carefully holding Flame's head so that it could not be raised as high as the stallion would have liked. The truck wasn't meant for hauling horses as tall as Flame. But there was no exchanging it now, and perhaps there was none other in the village that was more suitable anyway.

Steve remained with Flame for a long while, letting his horse look around to familiarize himself with his new surroundings. He gave Flame a little more line, so that the stallion might stretch his head a little higher and find out for himself just how far he could go. Soon Flame was content to keep his head lower than he usually carried it, and began sniffing the straw.

It was almost noon and Flame was back in his stall when Jay entered the shed, still in pajamas and bathrobe.

"Steve," he said, "you should have awakened me. I had no idea it was so late. I thought surely I'd hear you in the kitchen."

"I didn't go to the kitchen," Steve said.

"You mean you haven't eaten?"

"I haven't even thought about it."

"Then you come with me, and fast, Steve. This is no day to go without food! You'll need every bit of strength you possess. Come on, now."

Steve watched the small man in the bright blue bathrobe scurry to the door in his fast, bouncing gait. There Jay stopped. "Come on, Steve," he repeated. "We really haven't much time for all we have to do."

Steve followed him. That was just it . . . they didn't have much time. And that was why he couldn't eat at all.

OFF TO THE RACES

16

As the truck left the village the sky cleared and the sun made its appearance.

Jay, dressed as immaculately as on the day before, with his silver-headed cane on the seat beside him, drove faster and faster down the road. Without glancing back at the open window of the cab he said, "The sun's out, Steve!"

"Is it?" Steve couldn't tell much about the weather from inside the truck. He stood beside Flame, holding the lines tight for fear the stallion would raise his head too high and strike the roof again. As it was, Flame didn't like the semi-darkness of the truck nor the jostling they were taking over the bumpy road.

Jay called, "It'll mean a great crowd there to see you go."

The truck lurched and Steve had trouble keeping his feet. He touched Flame and found him sweaty from uneasiness, so he put the red cooler over him.

"Go slower," he told Jay angrily, "or no one will see us go! You're not driving a car."

"But, Steve, everyone drives this way. I watched very closely yesterday."

"Cubans aren't the best drivers in the world."

"They're not? You mean there are *other* ways to drive a car?"

"Slower ways," Steve said, still angry. "If you don't take it easier, Jay . . ."

"Now don't get mad, Steve. After all, I didn't know. *You're* the one who lives on this planet."

"Please go slower then," Steve repeated, "and miss the bumps. I'm having a hard enough time as it is keeping Flame still."

"Sure, Steve."

There was a slackening of speed and an end to the jostling. Steve stroked Flame's neck.

"All right back there?" Jay asked later.

"Much better," Steve answered.

"If there's anything else, just tell me, Steve. You must remember that all this is very new to me. But I enjoy driving. I really do."

Steve continued talking to Flame while listening to Jay. He didn't mind the man's incessant chatter. Anything was better than just waiting. It wouldn't be long now . . . an hour at the most, Jay had said.

"Even with the sun out it'll be a wet track," Jay called. "But I guess Flame won't mind, will he?"

"No, he won't mind."

Jay chuckled. "I don't imagine Kingfisher will like it, though. Their feet are weak enough without having to cope with such footing."

Kingfisher was the famed handicap champion from the United States, Steve recalled. Last night Jay had told him that this great horse would be in today's race. Steve had heard of Kingfisher long before he'd ever known Jay. At home one didn't read about racing without being aware of Kingfisher's unchallenged crown.

"This is a horse, not a bird," Steve reminded Jay.

"Oh, I know that, all right," Jay answered. "But there must have been some reason for naming him after a bird. Perhaps it was because of his feet, Steve. I'll know better when I see him."

Steve rubbed Flame's nose, and noticed that his hand was shaking a little. Sure, he was nervous. Wasn't it the most natural thing in the world to wonder if every move he made in the race would come instinctively, without thought or plan? It was no time to try to recall all he'd read about racing a horse, of blind switches and holes. Yesterday he'd been able to think, to plan. Today every attempt was futile, and his only hope was that it would be different once he rode Flame onto the track. He realized too that in spite of all the other horses and the great crowd, it would be, for him, the loneliest place in the world.

"Steve, Steve, what's the matter back there?"

"Nothing, Jay."

"You haven't answered any of my questions. You haven't said a word."

"I'm sorry."

"I was wondering if we couldn't go a little faster now. It's getting so late, and we don't have much time."

Steve listened to the wheels turning on the pavement, and wondered how long they'd been off the dirt road. "Sure, go ahead," he said. "But take it easy on the turns. And no sudden stops, Jay."

The truck lurched forward but Steve and Flame kept their feet. Jay talked of the great thrill it would be for him to watch the International. It would give him something to remember for a long, long time.

Steve was no longer listening to him. He heard only the hum of rubber tires, turning faster now, taking him and his horse closer and closer to El Dorado Park and all that awaited them.

Later came the sound of traffic on either side of the truck, and Steve knew they were approaching the city of Havana. The truck stopped often, only to plunge forward again. Jay had no feeling for the release of the clutch pedal.

Steve didn't go near the cab window. He did not want to see anything until it was time to leave the truck. It would be easier that way. He touched his face and wondered what he looked like. Jay had rubbed some kind of liquid over his skin and into his hair just before they had left. Steve turned his hands over, palms upward. These too Jay had treated, but only lightly. He hadn't rubbed the liquid in as he had done on Steve's face and scalp.

Steve noticed that while the color of his hands was the same as before, they had changed during the last hour. It seemed that they had grown, not in length but in breadth. He looked at them more closely and was sure of it. They were broad and flat with large knuckles, the hands of a man, not a boy . . . hands that had known many years of hard work.

Yet when Steve flexed his fingers they felt no different than before.

Again he touched his face, remembering Jay's words, "Take my word for it that no one will ever recognize you, Steve. It's important, of course, as they'll be taking pictures."

The truck swayed but Steve's hands remained on his face. He touched his nose. It was big, and the opening of his nostrils was large and round. His cheekbones seemed lower than they had any right to be, and there were deep lines in his face.

For a moment he was startled by the thought of what Jay must have done to him! Then Flame pushed his soft muzzle forward, and Steve realized that nothing about him had really changed as long as his horse knew him.

The truck stopped again, and while waiting for the traffic light to change Jay said, "We're almost at the track, Steve. Is everything all right?" Turning around, he looked through the cab window and studied the boy's eyes. Then he said, "Don't be concerned about how you look, Steve. It'll only last a few hours."

Steve said, "There's only one thing I'm concerned about, and it isn't my face."

Jay chuckled. "Don't worry about the race, Steve. Just get him out in front and keep him there."

"Sure," Steve said, "just like that."

The light changed and Jay was facing front again. "Just like that," he agreed.

The next time the truck stopped they were within El Dorado Park. Steve heard the neighs and nickers of horses and Flame became restless. The stallion's nostrils were spread wide, and when he screamed the shrillness of his whistle within the close confines of the truck was deafening.

"Easy, Flame," Steve said urgently.

But there was no quieting Flame now with the scent of other horses all around him. He tried to raise his head, and Steve had all he could do to keep him from striking the roof.

"Jay!" he called. "I must get him out of here soon." He wondered if he really expected it to be any easier once they were out of the truck.

"We're parked behind the barns, Steve. We must wait for Mr. Santos before unloading Flame. He wanted it that way."

The stallion moved uneasily beneath Steve's hands. "Don't you see Mr. Santos anywhere, Jay?" Steve asked impatiently. "Maybe he's forgotten all about us."

"No, not Mr. Santos, Steve. Don't worry so. We have five minutes before post time, and this is the way it was arranged. We're to make a dramatic entrance, Steve, after the introduction of the other horses. We're part of the show, and Mr. Santos won't forget us. He thinks of himself as being a superb showman."

Steve said bitterly, "Part of his show but not the race."

"Yes," Jay agreed, "that's about the way he figures it. Flame is to provide a bit of last-minute interest and color before the great race itself. After that we're not very necessary to Mr. Santos."

Flame gathered himself to rear, and Steve moved quickly, keeping him down.

"I do wish you'd come to the window and look at the crowd in the stands, Steve. I've never seen anything like it! And I believe . . . yes, the horses are now coming onto the track. Oh, I do hope Mr. Santos has *not* forgotten all about us! Perhaps we'd better unload Flame, Steve."

Steve heard the cab door open and then Jay called in relief, "Here comes Mr. Santos now. Are you all set, Steve?"

The tailgate was lowered and Steve led Flame toward it. He was set as he ever would be. The waiting was over. *Don't look at anyone but Flame. He's your only concern now.*

Flame followed him quickly off the truck, and Steve removed the red cooler, tossing it to Jay. He saw Mr. Santos step back hurriedly as Flame reared to his utmost height.

Steve knew that only then did the man realize what kind of a horse he had accepted for the International. The color of Flame's eyes changed to red at sight of the horses in the adjacent barns. And when he screamed his high-pitched clarion call of challenge, it carried beyond the stable area to the stretch where eight world-famous horses paraded to the post.

When the scream died down, Steve heard Mr. Santos blabbering wildly to Jay. But whatever he was saying went unheeded. Steve raised his knee to Jay's clasped hands and was boosted onto Flame's back. He gave Flame his head, and the stallion went forward eagerly, his bright eyes fixed on the parading horses.

Post Parade

17

High above Flame's craned head Steve saw the television cameras set up on the roof of the overflowing grandstand. He lowered his eyes, not wanting to look at anything but his horse and the track directly before them.

The footing was not as heavy as he had expected it to be after the long night of rain. The track had drained well, and that, together with a hot afternoon sun and the pounding hoofs of horses in preceding races, had made it a good track, almost fast.

He tried to pretend that he was back in Blue Valley. There was nothing ahead but a long run around the walled amphitheater of yellow, towering stone; they were alone except for the band of mares that would scatter at Flame's swift approach. If he could make believe it was that way, it would help. At least until they were off and running. Then he could let himself think of the race itself, hoping to make the right moves. If he could just get Flame out in front early, clear of all the other horses and running, then . . . yes, then there would be nothing to this race but a great red stallion.

Steve buried his head a little more in Flame's heavy mane, and he kept repeating, "Easy, boy. Easy now. There's no hurry. No hurry at all."

The sodden sand and clay slipped by in endless waves beneath the red stallion's ever lengthening strides. He snorted often but uttered no shrill call of angry defiance and challenge.

Steve took up more line, winding the reins about his fingers so they would not slip. Yet there was no slackening of Flame's strides, and Steve sensed in his horse a mounting eagerness to do battle with other stallions.

Steve's legs moved simultaneously with his hands and lips. "Around, Flame," he called. "All the way around."

He felt the tightening of Flame's muscles against the pressure of his legs. Flame knew what he was being asked to do, and still he did not respond.

Steve exerted more pressure with his legs, knowing that he could do no more than ask and then ask again. There was no forcing a horse like Flame. No battle of strength or wills. He could only hope that Flame would want to do what he asked of him. Their love for each other had to be greater than the stallion's wild instinct to fight. If not, the race would be over before it had begun, so far as they were concerned.

The first break in stride came with the sudden, metallic voice of the announcer over the public address system. The sound startled Flame, and Steve, taking advantage of this, was able to turn the stallion's head toward the outer rail.

The announcement was given first in Spanish, then in English. "Ladies and gentlemen, the horses are now approaching the starting gate," the announcer said. "Number One is Gusto from Italy. Number Two is Kingfisher from the United States. Number Three is Slow Burn, also from the United States. Number Four is Wellington from England. . . ."

Steve managed to turn Flame a little more. There was no lessening of the pressure of his legs or the urgency in his voice as he said softly, "Keep going, Flame. I want you all the way around."

The red stallion was in the center of the track, his strides slowing.

". . . Number Five is Tout de Suite from France. Number Six is Bismarck from Germany. Number Seven is El Chico from Chile. . . ."

Steve had Flame all the way around now, facing the backstretch again. "Good boy," he said. "Slow and easy now. We have lots and lots of time." He wanted to wait until the other horses were in their starting stalls, out of the way, making it easier for him to take Flame down to the gate.

"Number Eight," the announcer continued, "is Mister Tim from Ireland. Number Nine is . . ."

There was a pause and for an instant Steve stopped talking to his horse. *Here it comes,* he thought. *For the first time on any track. If they only knew . . . if they only knew!*

"Number Nine," the announcer repeated, "is Flame from the Windward Islands. He's been excused from the post parade and can be seen on the far turn. The horses are now in the hands of the starter, ladies and gentlemen, with one minute before post time."

Only the distant rumble of the tremendous crowd could be heard then. Suddenly above the roar Steve heard Jay's high-pitched voice calling him and then he saw the little man running across the track's infield. He had never seen Jay's legs move so fast before.

Nearing the rail, Jay shouted, "Go back and race, Steve. *Hurry!*" He waved his cane at them, and Flame, seeing it, shied across the track.

"Put your cane down," Steve called angrily. "I want to wait until the others are in the gate. It's the only . . ."

"I don't care what you've planned," Jay interrupted. "Don't keep them waiting a minute. Every second counts now. It's terribly important. Hurry, Steve, hurry!"

Steve got Flame over to the rail, and only then was he near enough to take a good look at Jay's face. First he was aware of nothing but a deep reddish color that distorted every feature. Then before his eyes Jay's face became nothing but a nebulous fiery swirl which spoke to him, the voice matching the terror that was in the blurred image. "You must hurry or I'll be left behind. . . ."

Steve was already turning Flame, and as he rode him away Jay's thought message reached him, as clear and distinct as his spoken words had been.

"I've heard from Flick. Something has happened, and the others are returning to the ship today. We're leaving, and if I shouldn't get back in time . . ."

The message faded, and Steve heard only the

increased pounding of Flame's hoofs as he urged him faster and faster toward the starting gate. Then suddenly Jay's thought message came again, fainter this time. "*I won't leave you here alone, Steve, but you must hurry, hurry, hurry. . . .*"

Steve leaned forward as his horse went into the turn. "Run, Flame, run!" he called, his own words echoing the urgency of Jay's message. He didn't want to be left behind, either!

Alongside the starting gate and just off the track, the official starter stood on a high platform watching the red horse come around the far turn. The man's heavy eyebrows swept upward in astonishment and then he shook his head. His voice was awesome and threatening as he called to a member of his ground crew, "Bert, go meet that fool rider! Slow him down!"

The starter turned back to the gate and to his immediate problem of quieting the horses which were already inside the stalls. The padded doors were being closed behind Gusto but the big brown gelding was trying to back out.

"Straighten his head, Cellini. Keep him in there," he barked through his amplifier to Gusto's rider.

The Italian jockey shouted back at him but the starter couldn't understand a word since Cellini spoke his native tongue. The starter turned his attention to the Number Five horse, the gray from France who was backjumping in back of the gate, refusing to go into the narrow alleyway that was his stall.

"Get that Tout de Suite horse inside, Joe," he rasped at another of his ground crew, "but don't upset him. Easy, now."

The French jockey was screaming something too, but as with Cellini the starter couldn't understand a word. He shrugged his shoulders in a gesture of helplessness, and wished that he had never taken this job of starting such a race. Back in the States he could keep jockeys in line, but not these jibbering riders who were supposed to understand and speak English, and didn't!

The jockey on El Chico was making as much noise as the rest of them and, of course, was speaking *his* language. The fellow up on Bismarck, the German horse, was the only quiet one in the bunch, and that included the two jocks from the States. But at least he could understand those two.

Braddish up on Kingfisher was screaming, "No chance! No chance!"

Of course there was no chance of his opening the gate yet. He had no intention of sending them off without that Number Nine horse. "Quiet!" he bellowed. "*I'll* do the talking!"

Anxiously the starter turned to see what was holding up Number Nine. The red horse had been brought to a stop by his rider a short distance away, and was now rearing high on his hind legs. The sight sickened the starter. No wonder Bert wasn't going any closer! The crewman, his arms raised high, stood in the middle of the track a good twenty feet away from the horse.

As if he didn't have enough trouble without *this*! the starter thought. He fingered the button that would cut the current from the magnets holding the front doors of the gate shut. All he had to do was to touch it and the race would be on without Number Nine.

He realized that the great stands were suddenly

quiet, so he was not alone in his amazement that the red horse should be here at all. Of course, that animal couldn't be what he looked like . . . a wild, unbroken stallion. Not here in such a race. He must be just part of the show, and a very spectacular show it had been with the field parading in the flag colors of their respective countries. But the starter was very tired of all these preliminaries. He wanted to send the horses off, as he'd been paid to do, and then go home.

"Bring that Number Nine horse down, Bert," the starter barked through the amplifier. "Don't be afraid of him." He had decided not to send the field off without the red horse. After all, difficult as the job might be, he had his reputation to maintain.

The more the starter looked at the red horse the more convinced he became that the animal was part of the show. A very beautiful horse, with fine classic features . . . too fine to be a race horse, really. He wore nothing but a rope hackamore with two long golden tassels hanging from it. His rider was sitting bareback and wore no silks, just T-shirt and jeans. Strange, very strange indeed. But the starter was not one to question what went on so long as there was no trouble at the gate. There was no doubt that this horse was being brought under control by his rider. However, he would like to have seen a bit in the stallion's mouth. He wished, too, that the jock would bring him down to the gate. Bert, apparently, wasn't going any closer in spite of his orders. He'd settle with Bert later.

Impatiently, the starter turned to one of the two red-coated outriders who had led the post parade before turning over the field to him and his crew. The nearer outrider was just beyond the gate, waiting to catch any runaway. The starter thought that he might just tell him to get that red horse down to the gate. However, he didn't have very much confidence in these track employees. Oh, the outriders tried hard enough and he supposed they had courage. But he doubted that they had the true *skill* to help out if trouble really started. It took a good horseman with many years of experience to stop a horse that was superior in speed to his own. Now back in the States he wouldn't have hesitated a moment to order an outrider after that red horse. He finally decided that if he was to get this race off at all, he'd better not hesitate here, either. Take a chance on the track's outrider. It was better than waiting any longer. He signaled to the man to bring the red horse down.

The starter watched the outrider go past the gate, eager enough but taking his horse along much too fast. He barked through the amplifier for him to slow down, and then finally to stop altogether.

The starter's bushy eyebrows had drawn together in dismay. He had seen something unexpected in the red horse, a wild, trembling eagerness to fight that hadn't been there before. "Forget him," he told the outrider, nervously. "Get your horse back and leave him alone."

When the outrider was safely away, the starter turned to the red horse again. He called to the hunched figure on the horse's back, "I'm sending them off! Bring your horse down, if you're going with them!" He used his most authoritative tone.

The starter watched the horse take a few steps forward. It was amazing enough that such a fractious animal was here at all, and more incredulous that his rider seemed to have him under some kind of control. The starter decided that he might get the field off without trouble if he put the red horse in the far end stall with three cages between him and the others.

As the red horse neared the gate, the starter could make out the jagged scars on his body. He took hold of his amplifier, clenching it hard. It couldn't be, of course! But where else would a horse get such scars but in battle with other stallions?

"Take that Number Nine horse to the stall at the very end!" he shouted to the rider. "Don't get him near the others!" His hand moved to the button that would open the stall doors. All he wanted to do was to start this race and catch the next plane home.

As Steve let the wet lines slip another inch between his fingers, and Flame approached the gate, he tried to keep the stallion's attention on the barrier, telling him that the narrow alleyway before them was no different from the passageways on Azul Island.

Flame suddenly stopped, fearful, Steve thought, of the wire-mesh door at the front of the stall. He pawed at the criss-crossed shadow it made on the track in back of the gate. Steve let him alone, glad that it was the mesh door that held Flame's interest and *not* the other horses. If he could only get him into the starting gate and then come out running . . .

A heavy silence had descended upon the stands and the track.

"It's only a shadow, Flame. See how that man walks right through it. But he won't come close to you. He won't lead you into the stall as he's done with the others. Don't look at him, Flame. Look only at the shadow, then at the stall. That's it. Go ahead now."

Flame chose to jump over the criss-crossed pattern rather than walk through it. His leap took him into the stall, and he stopped abruptly, startled by the wire-mesh door in front of him.

Steve comforted Flame as best he could, but actually he welcomed the close confines of the cage for, like the shadow, it alone now held the stallion's attention. And that was better than Flame's becoming aware of the horses in the stalls to his left.

He urged Flame a little closer to the wire door, and the stallion took a step forward, his head extended toward the screen, his nostrils flared and sniffing.

Suddenly from directly behind them came the heavy thump of the cage's back door being closed. Flame panicked at the loud noise. He reared and flung himself sideways against the padded stall. As he came down his forelegs struck the front door which gave easily as it was supposed to do in such emergencies. Startled by his easily won freedom, Flame reared again just as the starting bell rang and the other stall doors sprang open. From their cages emerged the famed horses of the world! The International had begun!

THE INTERNATIONAL RACE

18

Steve's every reflex was committed to keeping his seat as Flame twisted in midair, turning toward the sudden uproar on his left. When the stallion came down, Steve had urgent need for the bitless bridle. He pulled the reins hard, trying to straighten Flame's head and divert his attention from the onrushing field.

The horses swept past in the shape of a flying wedge, those late in breaking from the gate to the rear and jamming against each other while their jockeys screamed for racing room.

For a fraction of a second Flame stood flat-footed, his startled eyes following the tumultuous scene. He was aware of the pressure of hands and legs upon his body asking him to turn away, but above everything else he felt a mounting eagerness to do battle with those of his kind. He bolted after them, his shrill clarion call rising above the pound of many hoofs.

He did not rush headlong down the track. Instead his strides, while swift, were light and cautious. He continued screaming while waiting for one of the horses beyond to turn and accept his challenge. But they drew farther and farther away from him and he had to lengthen his strides. This caused his fury to mount still more, for he would have preferred that the fight be brought to him.

Steve knew that Flame had singled out the trailing gray horse to run down. He exerted more pressure, seeking to control his horse again. But Flame's ears remained flat against his head, and there was no change in the direction his long strides were taking him.

The stands began to slip by on their far right, but Steve was not aware of the roaring crowd. Only the trailing gray horse held his attention as he sought to prevent Flame's terrible onslaught of hoofs and teeth. His hands moved along the lines, constantly asking Flame to turn away. But the red stallion only leveled out still more.

The gray horse did not drop back as quickly as Steve had thought he would. In Blue Valley there was no horse to equal Flame's swiftness, but here it was different. For generations these horses had been bred for speed alone.

Steve sat back, not wanting to help Flame in his chase to run down the gray. They swept beneath the finish wire for the first time, with a mile of the race to go. Steve's hands and legs exerted more pressure on Flame, demanding now rather than asking. He had to get Flame to the middle of the track. Perhaps with no horse directly before him he would race!

But Flame knew no command but the one that came most inherently to him . . . to fight with teeth and hoofs, to kill or be killed! His strides came swifter and now he could almost reach his chosen opponent.

Steve mentally urged the gray on, at the same time trying desperately, with hands and legs, to break down the barrier of savagery that kept him from reaching Flame with his commands. He felt that if he were given just one slight opening he'd be able to control his horse again. He was certain that the bedlam at the start had so alarmed Flame that his horse wasn't even aware that he, Steve, was on his back!

When he was merely a stride's length behind the gray horse, Flame screamed again. Fury took hold of him when the gray did not even flick an ear in his direction. He stretched his head closer but his eyes were alert for any sudden move that might put him on the defensive. He drew alongside, wary now of the gray's hind legs. He hesitated a second, wondering why the other stallion did not turn upon him so they could rise together in deadly combat.

A pinpoint of hope glowed within Steve at Flame's hesitation. He felt Flame's bewilderment at the gray stallion's ignoring him so completely. He suddenly realized that Flame would find no *willing* opponent on this track, for the first and foremost instinct of these horses was to race, just as Flame's was to fight.

"Flame!" Steve called repeatedly into the flattened ears while his hands and legs worked harder than ever. If he could just get Flame's attention! But his horse plunged forward, seeking with bared teeth to tear and ravage the gray.

Steve saw the flaying whip of the gray horse's rider just before Flame was struck by it. Flame was so enraged he had eyes only for the horse. He wasn't even aware of the man who rocked on the gray's back, his leather whip moving rhythmically along his mount's side without touching him.

Flame thrust his head into this pendulum of hard leather. He felt the searing pain on his muzzle and drew back, more startled than hurt. Associating the unexpected blow with his opponent, he swerved abruptly away as he had done in countless battles, seeking time before attacking again.

His sharp turn took him across the track, bringing him face to face with an adversary so overwhelming that he forgot everything else in his sudden alarm. Tier upon tier before him rose a screaming mass of humanity!

Steve, too, seeking to regain his balance, saw the sea of faces in the grandstand. Their voices drowned out the plop of Flame's hoofs in the soft, moist dirt as the stallion plunged on in full flight. Then suddenly Steve was aware of the change that had come over Flame. He felt his horse's fear of the great crowd, and at the same time he saw the outer rail rushing to meet them.

He pulled hard on the left rein while his right hand slipped quickly across Flame's moving shoulder. He twisted his body, and for the first time since the race began Flame responded to his commands.

Without breaking stride Flame curved away from the stands and his speed blurred the faces of the spectators. Steve knew that Flame's fear had enabled him to break through the barrier that had kept them apart. Yet the streaming white rail came ever closer, matching the speed of Flame's swift turn. Steve bent more urgently to the left, seeking to narrow Flame's running arc and to avoid crashing into the rail.

When he was only inches away from it Flame straightened out, but like a magnet the rail held horse and rider close for another long stride. Then Steve saw the rail slip beneath his raised right knee, moving as though alive upon his horse's barrel. He felt the point of contact as soon as Flame did, the rail bending beneath the stallion's weight but not breaking. It seared the length of Flame's body before the stallion flung himself clear and bolted crazily toward the center of the track.

Steve made no attempt to stop him, knowing that his horse had not been injured, only burned by the friction of his running body against the wood. He tried to straighten Flame's zigzag flight down the track. Finally the stallion's head came up and there was a flick of the small ears when Steve called to him.

They approached the first of the long banked turns and Steve kept Flame high up on the graded dirt. He completely ignored the inner rail and the short inside way around the track, just as he ignored the racing horses far beyond. For flashing seconds he was aware only that Flame was listening to him again. It was as if they were back in Blue Valley, running for the sheer joy of running and being together. Steve rubbed Flame between the shoulder blades, then slipped forward and began asking him for more and more speed.

Back where the race had begun, the starter watched a tractor pull the gate from the track, leaving it clear for the horses when they came around again. That was the end of his job and he had little interest in the race itself.

He barely listened to the call of the announcer when the horses came off the first turn.

"That's Bismarck in front, followed closely by Slow Burn and Wellington. El Chico and Kingfisher are going wide. Mister Tim and Gusto are in a drive, coming up on the inside. Tout de Suite is . . ."

The sounds from the public address horn continued to crackle in the starter's ears but he didn't turn to the bunched field starting down the backstretch. Instead he walked across the track. Halfway to the outer rail he glanced toward the turn where the red horse which had caused all the trouble was being straightened out by his rider. Funny, that he should be watching him. Of course the horse wasn't going to get even a call. He was well out of the race already. That was the way the track officials had meant it to be, he supposed. The red horse had been asked here to put on a show, and he surely had obliged!

The starter's gaze followed the red horse, noting the way he stretched out going into the turn. No wasted effort there. He was really a very handsome horse, more beautiful by far than anything else on the track. But the starter remembered the scars on the stallion's red body and was glad that he had been successful in getting the race off without an accident. He could go home any time now.

His disinterested eyes turned to the racing field beyond. To him it was just another horse race, regardless of what they called it or had tried to make of it with all the dramatics beforehand. Oh, there was plenty of speed out there, a world of it, one might say, he decided. But after forty years in the business he'd seen the fastest horses there were. He recalled especially the match race in Chicago when the Black had beaten Sun Raider and Cyclone. After seeing that one he doubted that he'd ever be thrilled by another race.

He cast another look at the red horse, which was seemingly under control now and being taken high on the turn by his rider. Come to think of it, the horse reminded him a little of the Black. Same kind of wildness to his action that a domesticated horse never had. He was lengthening out yet holding his head high in pretty much the same way, too. But there was no comparison in speed. The Black would have been running the others to the ground by now while the red horse wasn't closing up any distance. Yet he wasn't falling back either, and that was surprising since he was only supposed to be part of the pre-race show.

The starter shrugged his heavy shoulders and continued across the track. Before reaching the outer rail he turned to watch the red horse once more. It was very unusual that he should be thinking of that Chicago match race here in Cuba years later.

Steve took Flame around the turn, his eyes sweeping over the field moving down the backstretch. No longer could he hear the roar of the crowd or anything else but Flame's hoofs lightly beating out a rhythm on the soft track. Suddenly the quiet was shattered by the call of the race announcer.

"Bismarck has increased his lead over Slow Burn, but on the far outside Kingfisher is moving up!"

Steve leaned more to the left, swaying with Flame into the graded turn. He took his horse over to the inner rail to save ground. He had never ridden Flame so fast *yet they were not overtaking the field!* Had he overestimated his horse's speed? Could a wild stallion compete with horses which had been bred through generations for racing speed alone?

"Run, Flame! Run!"

Steve listened to the stallion's snorts in response to his calls for more speed. He began pumping Flame with his legs, which he had never done before, and the snorts became louder. Only when they were on the straight-away did Flame quicken his strides. Steve felt the change that swept over the great red body when Flame saw the other horses far down the backstretch. He realized then what he had to do to make his horse run as he never had before.

"Go, Flame!" he screamed, kindling the fire of Flame's natural hatred for those of his kind, encouraging him to run the others down! Only by taking advantage of the generations of breeding behind Flame could he hope to make a race of it. He felt the growing heat of the reins while his own blood surged crazily, making him unmindful of the possible consequences of his act. His body and hands were never still, his voice never quiet. He had but one goal and that was to bring out every bit of speed the stallion possessed.

Flame listened to the never-ending calls urging him to catch up with those ahead. He felt the quickening beat of the hands upon his neck and the burning lines that kept his head straight. He lengthened his strides to keep time with the maddening rhythm on his back.

His eyes never left the horses which were now dropping back as he ran faster and faster. He selected an opponent. Just as he made his move to run him down there was a sudden twisting on his back. Then the lines seared his neck and he turned his head to relieve the pressure. Immediately his reddened eyes saw another horse still farther beyond. Again came the calls in his ear and the rhythmical beat of the hands against his body. He leveled out still more, needing greater speed to reach his newly selected opponent.

Steve waited until Flame neared the next horse, then once more he twisted on the stallion's back, throwing his weight heavily to the outside. The reins in his hands were like throbbing arteries through which coursed his blood as well as Flame's.

Steve straightened Flame's head so his horse could see the brown stallion running in the middle of the track. Every move was planned. He was encouraging Flame to attack and attack again while they went ever closer to the front.

The announcer said, *"Going into the far turn it's still Bismarck by three lengths. Kingfisher is on the far outside, passing Slow Burn and Wellington. Flame is now going up with Kingfisher...."*

The official starter had not left the track as he had intended doing. As though hypnotized, he had watched the beginning of Flame's mad rush down the backstretch. He had seen the huddled figure on the horse's back suddenly begin to rock wildly. Then the horse had exerted more speed, the rhythm of his strides finally matching that of his rider's movements. After that the rider had sat still, so still he seemed barely conscious of what was happening ... except at times. One of the times was when he had twisted his body as the red stallion overtook Mister Tim, another when the horse had sought to ravage Gusto and now when he had pulled him wide around the others and the red stallion was going after Kingfisher!

Steve watched the brown stallion drop back as those before him had done. He knew what he had to do again to get his horse away. He sat balanced, awaiting the precise second when by his weight and hands he could move Flame on to the last horse in front of them.

He saw Kingfisher begin to wobble and then bear out as they swept into the turn. Flame tried to swerve with him, but Steve had seen the opening left on the rail . . . and just beyond, three lengths away, was the leader, Bismarck! Steve moved quickly, tipping his weight to the inside and pulling hard on the left rein. Flame's head came around, and then the red stallion saw the running bay leader beyond!

Steve was taking Flame over to the rail when Kingfisher swerved back, closing the opening that had been there! Steve felt Flame gather himself to attack the horse before him. Desperately he threw his weight to the outside, and as his body and hands moved, Kingfisher suddenly stumbled and went down in a sprawling heap.

With the agility of one who has faced such emergencies in many battles, Flame avoided the fallen horse. He swerved, then jumped, twisting in the air. When he came down he sought to check his great speed in order to turn upon his beaten opponent. He felt the ground rise beneath his running feet, and then he saw the streaming outer rail which had caused him pain once before. In fear of it he quickly responded to the pressure upon his back to go on. He swept along the high banked turn and when the ground leveled out again he saw a lone horse running just beyond. His ears flattened in still another charge of relentless fury.

"In the homestretch," the announcer called, *"it's still Bismarck by four lengths. Flame is second. . . ."*

Steve heard the announcement but not the screams from the stands to their right. With each closing stride between the two stallions, he tried to decide what to do in this final run. His horse would catch up with Bismarck before the finish. But between the leader and the wire there was an empty track. What would happen when Flame saw no other horse beyond Bismarck? How could he get him to go on? If Flame hesitated or swerved to do battle with Bismarck the race would be lost.

Flame stretched his head, baring his teeth in his fury and reaching for Bismarck as he had done with the others. Steve slipped back in his seat, ready now to shift his balance and turn Flame away from Bismarck regardless of the outcome of the race. He gripped the reins tighter, and the heat coming from them seared his hands. He waited until Flame was close to the bay stallion's sweaty hindquarters and then he swayed far to the right.

Flame jumped away in quick response. His eyes were bright with anger and frustration as he sought still another horse upon which to vent his fury. But there was no horse beyond and to his right he heard the bedlam from the stands. He drew back before the frightening, ever mounting roar, seeking again the horse to his left.

Steve knew that what he had feared was happening. His horse was not going on! He took a fraction of a second to straighten Flame's head, keeping the stallion's eyes focused on the track. Suddenly there was a flash of red beyond the wire. *The crimson-coated outrider and his pinto horse had moved onto the track awaiting the finish of the race.*

Flame saw the outrider's mount and he swept forward eagerly, leaving Bismarck behind in great leaps. There was no slackening of his speed when he passed beneath the finish wire, for here at last was an opponent coming forward to meet him in combat!

THE END . . .

19

If the spectators had not known previously that they were witnessing the furious charges of an unbroken stallion, they were aware of it immediately following the end of the race. For the great red horse who had won surged past the finish line like a raging demon. They saw the object of his attack, for the outrider's pinto horse was rearing high in the air while his rider sought to take him off the track.

In silent horror they watched the distance close between the two horses. They saw the outrider slip from his saddle and vault the rail, leaving his horse alone to face the red stallion. They did not blame him for his fear.

Their eyes swept to the huddled figure on the back of the red horse as the jockey suddenly straightened, then twisted. They thought that he too would vault from his horse before the clash of bodies came. But he stayed on and they saw the quick movements of his hands.

The pinto horse came down, trembling in his fear,

then bolted for the paddock gate. The red stallion swerved, cutting off escape, and the pinto rose again, screaming in terror. The red stallion plunged forward, but before he reached his opponent, the crowd saw his rider move again. The stallion swerved abruptly away from the pinto, his strides coming long and fast as he swept down the track! In stunned silence the spectators watched him round the turn and go into the backstretch.

Suddenly a small, well-dressed man appeared on the track, waving his arms in front of the red horse and its rider. Impatiently the hushed spectators awaited an official explanation of what they had witnessed. When, instead, the red horse was taken out through the stable area gate and nothing was heard coming over the public address system, their voices broke as one and the great stands were no longer quiet.

The truck moved slowly through the stable area of El Dorado Park. Steve listened to the continuous roar of the crowd while pulling the red blanket over Flame's wet, trembling body.

"They'll follow us for sure," he told Jay through the open cab window.

"Let them," the man answered impatiently, "as long as they don't try to stop us. I won't tolerate any further delay."

Steve pulled the blanket high up on Flame's head and pinned it tight. "Will you be late?" he asked.

"I don't think so," Jay said. Then he added eagerly, "Oh, it *was* a race, Steve! There'll never be one to equal it. Nobody else could have ridden as you did today. No other horse could have run so fast. I scarcely believed

my eyes, Steve. I stood there stunned, forgetting everything but the sheer beauty of it."

Steve said nothing. Perhaps later he would see the
beauty of it, too. But not now. Nothing was real except
that they had won. He wanted only to be back in Blue
Valley.

The truck went faster once they were outside the
park. Steve steadied Flame, but did not tell Jay to slow
down. After a long while the man said, "I do wish I
didn't have to rush things so. The post-race ceremonies
would have been a lot of fun, Steve."

Steve remained silent.

"And the purse, that fifty thousand dollars . . . I
wish I could make it up to you. But I can't, Steve. I just
can't afford that much. Maybe you can claim the money
later?"

No, he'd never claim the purse at the risk of losing
something which to him was so much more valuable
than money. "It's not important," he told Jay.

"A nice way to look at it, but not very practical,"
the man answered. "However, it's strictly your decision
to make. I just regret that we didn't have the time . . ."

"I think it's better this way," Steve said. "Hurry up,
Jay."

Jay stepped more heavily on the accelerator. "I
guess you're right. Hold on now, Steve. We're outside
Havana and I'm really going to run this motor over."

City noises were left behind but there still remained the roar of many cars following them.

"Who's behind us, Jay?" Steve asked anxiously.

The man's gaze shifted to the side mirror. "Probably newspaper men and photographers," Jay answered. "At least I can see cameras in some of the open cars."

"They're not trying to stop us?"

"No, just staying with us, Steve."

Faster and faster went the truck. Steve steadied himself and Flame. Would they get back in time, if the big ship was to leave at sunset? He took a firm grip on the side rail as the floor heaved crazily beneath his feet.

Less than an hour of the day remained when Jay swung the truck around a sharp turn and went down the dirt road which led past the house and shed. Flame was knocked off balance by the bumpy road and when his head struck the roof he snorted in fury and pain. Steve comforted him without asking Jay to slow down, for behind them he could hear the screech of many tires rounding the turn. Soon now they would be face to face with their pursuers.

Finally the truck came to a stop, and when Jay lowered the tailgate Steve saw the taxicabs and cars parked behind.

"Bring him down as quickly as possible," Jay said. "Time's growing very short, Steve, and as much as I'd like to . . ." The newsmen surrounded him and he furiously pushed them away, his cane raised menacingly.

The newsmen fell back quickly but not because of Jay's threats of violence. They saw the blanketed red stallion come down the tailgate, his ears flat against his head and fire burning in his eyes at sight of them. Remembering all they had witnessed at the track, they made room for him. Where was this wild, unbroken stallion being taken? Stunned, they watched his small, meticulously dressed owner step from the road and start across an open field, closely followed by horse and rider.

They called to one another not to get too close to the horse, that he was being taken somewhere, and soon they'd know the answers to all their questions. Flash bulbs brightened the day as photographers stopped to take pictures of this weird chase of the winner of the International. The story that was unfolding would be far more interesting to their readers than the race itself! Knowing this, they were content to wait.

They entered a rather dense woods and, using the trees for protection against any possible attack by the red horse, drew a little closer. Finally they saw a clearing just beyond. They looked for a farm. Certainly the end of the chase had to be here!

Their steps slowed when they stepped into the clearing, for they did not like to leave the protection afforded them by the trees. They came to an abrupt stop when the small owner ceased running. They saw him turn to his horse and rider, then he waved his hand in the air . . . and there were those among them who said later that they heard a soft whirring noise at that moment. They didn't go any closer.

Flashlight bulbs popped as the photographers took advantage of the few precious seconds in which to shoot pictures. When the barrage of light was over, the clearing was empty.

For a moment the newsmen stood in stunned, shocked silence. Then one of them walked forward, stopped in the middle of the clearing and continued on, finding nothing. The others turned to one another, still silent and unmoving, their eyes asking questions they could not ask aloud . . . and there were no answers.

Miles upon miles above the clearing, Steve Duncan sat in the cruiser and was as silent as the newsmen they had left behind.

"Comfortable, Steve? I'm trying to give you as much room as possible after all your hard work."

"Yes, thanks." He saw the flaming backdrop of the sun out the window. He might have been sitting by himself in outer space, except that there was no rush of air, no ripping, sucking void, nothing but deathly quietness and finally the revolving heavens. They must be turning now.

Jay spoke again, his voice less grim than it had been below. "I'll get back in time, Steve, just a matter of a minute or so now."

Steve said nothing.

"I won't forget that race," Jay went on. "I've never seen such speed!"

Steve remained silent, and finally Jay said, "You're wondering why I should be so impressed by a horse's speed when we're traveling pretty fast right now, aren't you?"

"Yes, I am."

The man chuckled. But there was no laughter in his voice when he said, "Don't envy our perfection of mass acceleration, Steve. Sure, there's no place in the universe we can't go, but actually you should feel sorry for us."

"Sorry?" Steve asked.

"Sorry," Jay repeated. "Perhaps your people won't make the same mistake we did, but most likely they will. We perfected so many startling things, Steve, that in our haste and eagerness to get on we left behind something pretty valuable in itself. You have one of them standing right beside you."

The heavens began to move faster and Steve knew they had begun their descent. "Flame?" he asked. "Are horses what you mean, Jay?"

"Not only horses, Steve," Jay answered quietly, "but *all* animals."

Steve saw the Caribbean Sea rushing to meet them, then the glowing patch on the water, even before he could make out Azul Island.

"We're not the same without animals," Jay continued, "although many of us are inclined to think so; Flick is one. Oh, it's not what you may think of as my selfish interest in the race horse that prompts me to say this. For generation upon generation I've seen what's happening to our young people. They need animals desperately."

Steve felt Jay's hand on his arm. "Don't envy us our ships of metal, Steve. Your love for Flame and his love for you go far beyond anything that we have to offer our young people. Young hands such as yours that can calm a frightened animal are the beginning of better worlds for all of us. It's love without selfishness, and by achieving such a state you and your people are well on your way. I earnestly hope that you'll never go astray as we did, traveling the bright, gay avenues that consist only of material things."

"Will I see you again?" Steve asked.

"I don't know, Steve. It will be a long, long time, if I do return."

"In your time or mine, Jay?"

"Yours, of course, Steve. It won't be long for me. You wouldn't even notice any change in me. But you . . ."

"Yes, Jay? Will I be an old man?"

"Pretty old, Steve," Jay replied quietly.

Azul Island had emerged from the sea, a speck, a dot, then the walls of Blue Valley enveloped them. As Steve's body swayed, Jay spoke. "It's just as easy for me to drop you off here, Steve. You've had a hard day, and I'll see that your launch gets back. I still have time for that."

All was quiet again. Steve felt Jay's hand on his arm, helping him to his feet.

"Out with you now," Jay said with feigned lightness. "We must part for a little while."

"A little while, Jay? It won't be a little while at all. It'll be a long time . . . a long, long time!"

"You're tired and upset, Steve," Jay's voice came from a great distance. "I've asked too much of you these last few days. You'd better rest. Here's a good spot. Stretch out now. Take it nice and easy, Steve. That's it, go to sleep now . . . go to sleep. . . ."

...And the Beginning

20

Steve Duncan opened his eyes to find his hands clasped beneath his head while he lay on the ground. A long blade of succulent grass was between his lips and he removed it, wondering when he'd put it there. The waterfall droned behind him and some of the mares nickered. Foals answered in high-pitched, wavering neighs.

He looked at the sky. It was well past sunset but the brilliant afterglow still colored the clouds.

Jay and his friends would be gone by now. Steve sat up, turning again to the sky, wishing he could have seen their ship rise from this world. But then Jay had said it glowed only when landing. So even if he'd stayed awake he wouldn't have seen it.

Getting to his feet, he found Flame with the band. His horse wore neither the red blanket nor the bridle, so Jay had taken those with him. Disappointment flared in Steve's eyes, for he would have liked to keep the hackamore. Then Jay would have been with him always, regardless of the light years and endless space which separated them.

He called to Flame, wanting to make certain his horse had suffered no injuries from the race and trip. There was no sign of lameness or injury in the stallion when Flame came to him at a fast walk. In fact Flame looked so fresh and eager that it seemed to Steve he could have raced again, at that very moment, with no trouble at all.

Steve walked around his horse, finding no caked dirt or mud from the track on the red body. He picked up the oval-shaped hoofs and found them clean also. Quickly he went to Flame's right side again, searching for evidence of the long burn from the outer rail. Here too he was disappointed, finding nothing but the jagged scars he had known before.

Flame looked as if . . . yes, he looked as if he had not raced at all!

Steve turned quickly away from Flame, and the first light of uncertainty appeared in his eyes. He climbed the trail as fast as his legs would carry him, stopping only at the ledge to grab a flashlight and go on. Upon reaching the tunnel he went inside, his strides coming faster than he'd ever traveled the underground world. Finally he reached the slits in the far western wall of Azul Island. He looked hard and long, searching but finding nothing except the flat, still surface of the Caribbean Sea. He rushed headlong through the tunnels again, telling himself that he hadn't really expected to find the white patch on the water. The big ship had left at sunset.

When he arrived back at the ledge he went first to the box in which he kept the empty food tins before burying them. But once there he turned quickly away, telling himself there was no way of gauging if the box was any more full than when he had left with Pitch for Antago. Burying the cans was one of the jobs he had meant to do immediately upon his return.

When *had* he returned . . . days ago? . . . or an hour ago? He remembered stretching out on the grass, looking up at the sky that was so spotted with small, fleecy clouds. He hadn't wanted to fall asleep. But had he slept after all? Was this the very same day? Were Jay and Flick and their ship nothing but a fantastic dream that had included racing Flame?

He moved quickly to the rear of the cave to get Pitch's can of tea. He looked at it, wondering exactly how much tea Pitch had left there. Jay and Flick had liked their tea strong, so he must have used a lot. Or had he? There was no way of being sure.

The can dropped from his hands and he ran down the trail, calling to Flame at the top of his voice. The stallion came from the nearby pool at his call, and Steve mounted him quickly. Then he rode down the valley, feeling the surge of muscles that carried him along at greater and greater speed. Flame could *not* have raced only a few hours before and go so fast now! A numbness swept over Steve, yet he continued taking his horse through the marsh and gorge and finally across the smaller valley.

He slid down from Flame's back at the entrance leading to the sea chamber and ran inside. Reaching the chamber he stopped abruptly when he saw the launch gently rocking in the waters of the canal. But then, he had expected to find it there. Jay had said he would return it. He moved forward slowly, his eyes on the ropes that held the *Sea Queen* to the wooden pilings. Here he would have his final answer, for no one tied knots exactly the way he did. If Jay had returned the launch, the knots would be different.

Steve went from one rope to the next, examining each a long, long time. Finally in a dazed stupor he left the chamber and returned to Flame.

Night had come to Azul Island. Yet Steve made no attempt to mount his horse. He merely stood beside him, looking up at the stars.

It was the same day, the very day he had told himself to stop daydreaming of racing Flame. He had gone to sleep, to dream the most fantastic dream of all!

Suddenly he laughed at the thought of how ridiculous he had been to think it might be true.

"Come on, Flame," he said sadly. "Let's go back."

He rode at a slow gallop, his eyes turning often to the night sky as the stars grew in number, millions upon millions, and millions more. Yet Jay had said they were nothing compared to what lay beyond.

"What a very silly person I am, Flame," Steve said, "to keep thinking about a man I made up in a dream."

Flame tossed his head and snorted as if in complete agreement. Steve grinned and sent the red stallion into a hard run, for what he had in reality was far better than anything a dream could offer.

EPILOGUE

In the Reading Room of the New York Public Library a thin, wiry man removed his steel-rimmed glasses and softly pressed his eyeballs to help relieve the strain of a long day of research. Finally he looked around the large, quiet room and rose to his feet, closing his books and picking up his notes. He went to the desk in the center of the room, very careful to keep from rustling his papers so as not to disturb the other readers.

"I didn't quite finish today, Ray," he told the young man behind the desk, "so I'll take this one home."

The librarian smiled and said, "You've said that every day for the past week, Mr. Pitcher. Why don't you see something of New York tonight instead of working?"

The man called Pitcher met the librarian's smile with grave seriousness. "I couldn't find anything so fascinating as this," he said, gesturing toward the book. "And I wish you'd stop calling me Mr. Pitcher, Ray. It's *Pitch.*" He laughed. "I don't answer to anything else, and we've known each other a whole week."

The librarian pushed the book across the desk. "All right, *Pitch*. See you tomorrow then."

Pitch left the room and went down the winding marble steps without waiting for the elevator. He held the book close to his thin chest thinking how little Ray must know about Spanish-American history to believe *anything* in New York could be as interesting. Why, nothing could be so exciting as reading about those Spanish conquests! There was no doubt that the Spaniards had used Azul Island as a supply base. He'd found that out for sure. Oh, he'd have a lot to tell Steve, all right. He was being very well rewarded for this long trip.

Outside the library he paused on the steps, almost frightened by the scurrying horde of people on their way home from work. He was finding it difficult to get used to all this confusion and rush after his life on Antago and with Steve in Blue Valley.

He watched the seemingly endless crowd at the newsstand below as commuters picked up their evening papers and then disappeared into the subway entrance with scarcely a pause. He held his book a little closer.

He passed the stand with no intention of buying a paper. But suddenly he was being pushed by the mob and he found himself directly in front of the stand. A folded newspaper was thrust in his hand.

"I don't want it," he said politely.

The newsman continued handing out papers, but his eyes kept shifting back to the customer who hadn't paid. "Come on. Come on," he said impatiently. "Evenin' papers . . . *Journal, Post, Telly* . . . Here y'are . . .

C'mon, Mister, pay up . . . Papers, get your evenin' papers . . . *Journal, Post* . . ."

Afraid that he might be jostled again and that his glasses might fall off and break if he remained in front of the crowded stand any longer, Pitch paid for the newspaper and allowed himself to be pushed to the sidewalk. There he safely avoided the subway entrance and walked quickly down the street to the nearest public waste receptacle. He began to stuff the newspaper inside.

Suddenly he stopped, his attention caught by the front-page picture of a horse and rider. For a long while he just stared at it in dazed bewilderment, then he withdrew the paper and unfolded it.

The caption beneath the picture read:

Fifty-thousand-dollar purse still unclaimed by the owner of winning horse in yesterday's International Race at Havana, Cuba. Mystery deepens as newsmen state that horse, rider and owner disappeared before their eyes in an open clearing during chase immediately following the race. Equally astounding is that no racing association has the registration of a horse named Flame, yet he defeated eight of the world's best! Who is this horse? Where is he?

Up the crowded street Pitch ran, talking aloud to himself, yet no one paid him the slightest attention.

"*It's Steve's Flame,*" he said. "*There's no mistake about that. So it has to be Steve riding him. But what has the boy done to his face? How on earth did he and Flame ever get to Cuba? What's going on back in Blue Valley? Steve, Steve, what in the world has happened? Who is that small man standing beside you?"*

Pitch turned into the airlines terminal, carrying only the day's newspaper, for his book on the past had been dropped and forgotten long minutes before.

About the Author

Walter Farley's love for horses began when he was a small boy living in Syracuse, New York, and continued as he grew up in New York City, where his family moved. Unlike most city children, he was able to fulfill this love through an uncle who was a professional horseman. Young Walter spent much of his time with this uncle, learning about the different kinds of horse training and the people associated with them.

Walter Farley began to write his first book, *The Black Stallion*, while he was a student at Brooklyn's Erasmus Hall High School and Mercersburg Academy in Pennsylvania. He eventually finished it, and it was published in 1941 while he was still an undergraduate at Columbia University.

The appearance of *The Black Stallion* brought such an enthusiastic response from young readers that Mr. Farley went on to create more stories about the Black, and about other horses as well. In his life he wrote a total of thirty-four books, including *Man o' War*, the story of America's greatest thoroughbred, and two photographic storybooks based on the two Black Stallion movies. His books have been enormously popular in the United States and have been published in twenty-one foreign countries.

Mr. Farley and his wife, Rosemary, had four children, whom they raised on a farm in Pennsylvania and at a beach house in Florida. Horses, dogs and cats were always a part of the household.

In 1989 Mr. Farley was honored by his hometown library in Venice, Florida, which established the Walter Farley Literary Landmark in its children's wing. Mr. Farley died in October 1989, shortly before the publication of *The Young Black Stallion,* the twenty-first book in the Black Stallion series. Mr. Farley co-authored *The Young Black Stallion* with his son, Steven.

**THE EXCITING TALE
OF HOW STEVE MET FLAME**

THE ISLAND STALLION

Steve Duncan had a haunting vision of finding a magnificent red stallion . . . and finally discovered him in a hidden island paradise. But the giant horse was wild and unapproachable. Then Steve saved Flame from a horrible death, and a miraculous friendship began—changing *both* their lives forever.

**A THRILLING SAGA OF DANGER
ON AZUL ISLAND**

Flame faces a vicious new enemy! The giant red stallion is used to fighting horses—his leadership of the wild band on the remote island has been tested again and again. But never before has he been threatened by people. Now a greedy and violent man is coming after the unwary stallion . . . determined to break his body *and* his spirit!

**TWO GREAT HORSES
MEET FOR THE FIRST TIME!**

When their plane crashes in the Caribbean Sea, Alec and the Black are swept apart. The exhausted stallion is carried by the currents to a remote island. There he finds a herd of wild horses ruled by the giant red stallion Flame. But before the Black and Flame can determine which is the dominant male, they must fight a rabid vampire bat intent on destroying the entire herd.

**FLAME WILL GIVE THE BLACK
THE RACE OF A LIFETIME!**

THE BLACK STALLION CHALLENGED!

Steve Duncan has claimed that his horse, Flame, is faster than the Black. And when Flame and the Black had their first run together, Alec had to admit that the Black might have met his match. Now that the two stallions are meeting in a major race, the whole *world* wonders if the Black can hold his own against the upstart challenger. . . .

**DON'T FORGET THE STORY
THAT BEGAN IT ALL. . . .**

THE BLACK STALLION

Alec Ramsay first saw the Black Stallion when his ship docked at a small Arabian port on the Red Sea. Little did he dream then that the magnificent wild horse was destined to play an important part in his young life; that the strange understanding that grew between them would lead through untold dangers to high adventure in America.

**AN EXCITING RACING STORY
WITH THE BLACK'S OLDEST FILLY**

Can a filly win the Kentucky Derby? That's what Henry Dailey hopes when he buys the Black Stallion's filly. But Black Minx has a mind of her own. Her desire to go fast is great, but so strongly does she resist training that Alec and Henry have to trick her into running! As they bring her to Churchill Downs for the great race, they wonder if she truly is up to the challenge.

**NO ONE CAN WRITE A RACING ADVENTURE
LIKE WALTER FARLEY.**

When Hopeful Farm burns down, Alec Ramsay's
dreams for the future go up in smoke. To make matters
worse, a strong young colt named Eclipse is threatening
to replace the Black in the hearts of racing fans. The
Black is getting older, and no one believes that he could
win again. No one, that is, but Henry Dailey. Against
all odds, Henry and Alec create a sensation as they
bring the Black back to the track—and the crowd
knows that they are about to watch the race of the
century!

HOW MUCH DO YOU KNOW
ABOUT HARNESS RACING?
MEET A NEW HERO, AND A FASCINATING SPORT!

THE BLACK STALLION'S BLOOD BAY COLT

Young Tom Messenger has been taking care of Bonfire, the second son of the famous Black Stallion, since his birth. Tom has earned the trust of Jimmy Creech, the veteran driver who owns Bonfire, and Tom is eager to work with the young colt, building his strength and endurance. But suddenly Jimmy's health takes a bad turn and Tom must take the reins himself. The horse is a natural, but Tom doesn't know the first thing about harness racing. And he'd better learn fast. . . .

If you loved
this story...

Collect all of the horses from
Breyer's Series for young readers!

Breyer Animal Creations' model horse and book series includes: *The Black Stallion* and *Flame, The Island Stallion*. Read them both and collect the models!

Collectible!

To see the complete line of Breyer model horses and accessories and to find a store near you, visit our website at:

www.BreyerHorses.com

To receive a free mini-catalog and an issue of Breyer's *Just About Horses* magazine (dedicated to model horses and the real horses that inspired them), please write:

Breyer® Animal Creations®
14 Industrial Road, Dept. RH • Pequannock, NJ 07440